"I'll take you

Aristide addressed her rigidly, then turned back as she reached the front door.

"No, thanks." And with that calm retort, Tabby walked out of his penthouse apartment and finally felt able to breathe again.

"Tabitha..."

She turned her tousled head and arrowed glacial blue eyes back at him as she awaited the elevator.

"If there *should* be consequences—"

"Forget it," Tabitha murmured pleasantly. "I wouldn't come begging to you if I was down to my very last penny and *starving*. That's a promise."

A dramatically shocking Harlequin Presents duet from Lynne Graham.

Billion-Dollar Bride Swap

Wrong wife! Right billionaire?

Sisters Violet and Tabitha are desperate to fund life-saving medical treatment for their mother. So, when their estranged grandfather agrees to give them a lump sum *if* one of them marries the billionaire who's key to his next business deal, Tabitha says yes to becoming a stranger's convenient bride. Until she shockingly discovers that she's pregnant, and Violet must take her place at the altar!

Walk down the aisle with...

Violet and Tore's story
Unveiling the Wrong Bride

Tabitha and Aristide's story
Her Two Greek Secrets

Both available now!

HER TWO GREEK SECRETS

LYNNE GRAHAM

PRESENTS

If you purchased this book without a cover you should be aware that this book is stolen property. It was reported as "unsold and destroyed" to the publisher, and neither the author nor the publisher has received any payment for this "stripped book."

Recycling programs for this product may not exist in your area.

ISBN-13: 978-1-335-21365-5

Her Two Greek Secrets

Copyright © 2026 by Lynne Graham

All rights reserved. No part of this book may be used or reproduced in any manner whatsoever without written permission.

Without limiting the exclusive rights of any author, contributor or the publisher of this publication, any unauthorized use of this publication to train generative artificial intelligence (AI) technologies is expressly prohibited. Harlequin also exercises their rights under Article 4(3) of the Digital Single Market Directive 2019/790 and expressly reserves this publication from the text and data mining exception.

This is a work of fiction. Names, characters, places and incidents are either the product of the author's imagination or are used fictitiously. Any resemblance to actual persons, living or dead, businesses, companies, events or locales is entirely coincidental.

For questions and comments about the quality of this book, please contact us at CustomerService@Harlequin.com.

TM and ® are trademarks of Harlequin Enterprises ULC.

Harlequin Enterprises ULC
22 Adelaide St. West, 41st Floor
Toronto, Ontario M5H 4E3, Canada
www.Harlequin.com

HarperCollins Publishers
Macken House, 39/40 Mayor Street Upper,
Dublin 1, D01 C9W8, Ireland
www.HarperCollins.com

Printed in Lithuania

Lynne Graham was born in Northern Ireland and has been a keen romance reader since her teens. She is very happily married to an understanding husband who has learned to cook since she started to write! Her five children keep her on her toes. She has a very large dog who knocks everything over, a very small terrier who barks a lot and two cats. When time allows, Lynne is a keen gardener.

Books by Lynne Graham

Harlequin Presents

Two Secrets to Shock the Italian
His Royal Bride Replacement
Shock Greek Heir

Cinderella Sisters for Billionaires

The Maid Married to the Billionaire
The Maid's Pregnancy Bombshell

The Diamond Club

Baby Worth Billions

The Diamandis Heirs

Greek's Shotgun Wedding
Greek's One-Night Babies

Billion-Dollar Bride Swap

Unveiling the Wrong Bride

Visit the Author Profile page
at Harlequin.com for more titles.

CHAPTER ONE

Aristide Romanos, billionaire entrepreneur, was relieved when his senior PA, Georgio, contrived to give him a slight smile from his hospital bed. 'Only one more scan to go and I'll be free to leave, sir.'

Aristide winced. He wasn't always the most considerate employer but even he was not about to drag an employee with a broken ankle straight out of hospital. 'No, you won't be. You'll stay here until a medic tells you to leave and then only to return to the hotel where you will rest.'

A car crash in the airport car park had taken out Aristide's entire personal team of six. Three were down with concussion, one with a broken arm and another with a mix of injuries. Currently, Georgio was the only member of his staff to remain in full possession of his wits.

'But, sir...what will you—?'

'I will proceed to Traxis.' Aristide paused to enjoy Georgio's look of disbelief. 'I *can* work alone. I will do a tour and meet senior personnel. Another team will arrive to assist me tomorrow. Relax, Georgio, you're on sick leave.'

Aristide knew that his PA didn't find it any easier to relax than he did. Georgio, like Aristide, was a driven type-A personality. Ignoring the attention that his six-foot-four-inch, well-built frame and sleek, dark good looks garnered from the female staff, he strode out of the private hospital and back into his limo, directing his driver to his destination. Another takeover, another day, he reflected wryly, but, undeniably, work was the spice of life to him.

He scanned a text from a former lover and without hesitation asked her to lose his number. He was only twenty-eight but he didn't do repeats with women, never had, never would. Sex was just sex, a necessity for a male of his appetites, but it could still be controlled within certain boundaries. An entire weekend was as close as Aristide got to commitment. He was a shameless playboy, fashioned that way from growing up with a father who couldn't resist women. Ex-wives, ex-partners and discarded lovers and children had littered his father's life.

That kind of background left scars that Aristide was fully aware of having. But, even so, he simply didn't want female drama in his life: no broken hearts, no accusations of infidelity, no jealous scenes, no betrayals, no lies. Aristide could not imagine having only *one* woman in his life and he was even less keen on the option of ever fathering a child of his own.

Without a doubt, his last will and testament would spread his wealth across the best of his many relatives.

One month later

Tabby checked the test and imagined her eyes shooting out wide on stalks like a cartoon character telegraphing fear and alarm. Her blood ran cold in her veins, shock rippling through her. She was *pregnant*. She sucked in a deep breath to ward off the dizziness assailing her. How on earth could she have been so stupid? So reckless? She, who prided herself on her intelligence and self-discipline, had just utterly messed up her life *and* her poor sister's. At the eleventh hour, she would have to back out of the business marriage she had contracted to complete and her twin, Violet, would have to take her place.

And that was only the *first* of the mistakes she had made, she acknowledged wretchedly. She had messed up so badly that she was horribly ashamed of herself. Furthermore, now she would have a child to raise alone, a baby who would be totally dependent on her currently useless self!

How on earth had she contrived to sink so low, so fast?

And the memories began to flutter back in a series of episodes like some ghastly soap opera…

It had started with their mother, Lucia's illness, persistent cancer, which had dogged her for many years and right then their beloved mum had been at her last post. Her sole hope for survival was a new experimental drug on a clinical trial in the USA. But it cost money to get a place on such trials and one thing Lucia and her two daughters had never had was surplus cash.

Indeed the only wealthy person they even knew, and they scarcely *knew* him, was their grandfather, Tomaso Barone, he of the hard heart who had cast off their mother when she was a teenager who chose to marry the wrong man. And regrettably, Sam Blessington, their father, had been very much the wrong man, a feckless artist with a taste for booze, violence and other women and no interest at all in his twin daughters. Throughout their childhood there had been sobering experiences like bailiffs, homelessness and hunger and, on several occasions, Lucia had begged her father to help them. But not *once* had he come through for his estranged only child. So, when Violet and Tabby had made an appointment to meet Tomaso and ask for his financial assistance to enable their mother to get on that trial, they had not been optimistic.

It had been a huge shock when Tomaso had looked across his giant office desk and said, 'Yes, I will help your mother *this* time...if in turn one of you does something for me.'

'Anything!' she and Violet had promised simultaneously with no idea whatsoever of what he had been about to propose: a marriage with the heir to his rival competitor's company to cement a business deal.

'As your sister has a child, it will obviously be you,

Viola, who takes up this wonderful opportunity,' her grandfather had insisted. He wasn't even aware that she was called Tabitha because her drunken father had bungled registering their birth names. On paper she was Viola Tabitha but in actuality she had always gone by her middle name.

Of course, there had been no choice but to agree, not when he had been dangling the bait of that all-important cash for their mother's benefit. The very belief that his grandchild would get to wed the super-rich heir to Renzetti Pharmaceuticals and carry on what he somehow deemed to be *his* legacy had delighted the older man. Neither Violet nor Tabitha had guessed that, when it came to actually handing over the money, he would welch on the deal with the excuse that they had to wait longer for it.

Only they hadn't *had* time to wait when their mother was so frail and instead Tabby had had to ask her future husband's lawyers for the sum as conditional on her signing the pre-nup before the wedding. And in return, she had been asked to reduce the five-year marital term to three instead and of course she had agreed, not wanting to have her own life derailed for any longer than necessary.

Consenting to marry a male who couldn't even be bothered to meet her prior to the wedding had freaked Tabby out. It had felt as though every one of her personal choices was being stolen from her: she was to marry a stranger and live in his home and put up with whatever he chose to throw at her for three long endless years. A prison camp had sounded more appealing than that, especially after she had read the clause relating to her personal behaviour, which barred her from meeting any men or consorting with them in any way.

Why? Tabby had never had a man in her life or particularly *wanted* one. Her father had for ever soured her on the male sex but, even so, she still hadn't liked being a virgin at almost twenty-two. She'd seen that as a rite of passage into adulthood that she hadn't wished to wait another three years to experience. A mere physical thing, a bodily thing, and not something to make a big deal about, she had decided, in her innocence.

And that decision, Tabby recognised, and that rash attitude had brought her to her current crisis of having conceived an unplanned child. It should have been something she could celebrate and she blamed *him* for the fact she couldn't because *he* had already accused *her* of trying to set him up when the condom failed. What kind of madness had possessed her when she'd thought that she could have a simple one-night stand as other women did? Well, for her, it had gone badly wrong and she blamed inexperience and her ignorance in bedding such a dreadful choice of a guy for the consequences.

Certainly, the day it had happened, she had had no idea of what lay ahead. It had begun as a normal shift in her office temp job in a large insurance company where she worked for Ed Stokes, a harmlessly inefficient middle manager, who was, nonetheless, related to the CEO, who absolutely never showed his face in the building.

'Julian…' aka, the CEO of Traxis '…suggested that I look after this senior audit chap coming in,' Ed had explained. 'But I want you to do it instead because you have a degree in accounting and I work in sales.'

There had been no point reminding Ed that Tabby hated accounting and had learned that any day she preferred general office admin to perusing profit and loss figures. Ed was the boss and she had an easy job as long as she took care of all the many things that intimidated mild-mannered, socially awkward Ed, like meeting new people or dealing with senior staff. He shunted off everything he disliked onto Tabby and he got away with it too because he was on first-name terms with the big boss.

Tabby had hung about Reception awaiting the arrival of the VIP accountant with nothing but the name of the company he worked for in terms of information: Millwright and Sons.

A very tall, commanding male with a shock of cropped black curls had entered and the receptionist had greeted him while Tabby had hovered uncertainly by her side, sheltering behind the desk the more she noticed about the new arrival. The fabulous custom fit of his black suit, the unusual formality of the silk tie and closed collar on his shirt, the reality that he was so tall she had to crane her neck and tip her head back even to steal a look at his lean, bronzed face.

'Mr Millwright?' the receptionist asked hesitantly.

The reference to his London audit team, who wouldn't be arriving until the next day, relaxed Aristide into the belief that he was expected.

'No, I'm Aristide Romanos,' he announced.

'I'm Tabitha Blessington, Mr Romanos…' another voice interposed and he turned his proud dark head to look at her. 'My boss asked that I show you around.'

Aristide was taken aback that the CEO was not in place to greet him but, as a male, he was immediately captured by the angelic fairness of the speaker. Aristide liked blondes, he always had, but rarely had he met one quite so beautiful, who had not plundered every cosmetic trick in the box. This one had flawless translucent skin like fine china and not even a trace of lipstick on her sensually plump lips. Not to mention huge blue eyes, perfect features and a mane of pale blonde hair that looked as natural as a child's. She had an unspoilt look new to his experience and it grabbed his interest, which would at best be…fleeting, he assumed without a doubt of that in his handsome head. An arrogance taught by countless very willing ladies in his past.

He didn't view her as an employee. He owned dozens of companies. He took them over and sorted out their issues before installing trusted executives. He might well never visit Traxis Insurance again, so he didn't consider himself bound by any rules of the workplace.

'Miss Blessington,' Aristide returned as she extended a slender hand to his much bigger paw, the size differential between them making his shapely mouth quirk with amusement. She was small and unexpectedly slight with fewer curves than was usually his preference but his interest abated not a jot.

'Tabitha…or, er… Tabby will do,' she heard herself say like a woman in a dream because he was truly the most gorgeous male she had ever met and she felt overwhelmed by his presence. As if that were not bad enough, a sensation like an electric shock tremored down her arm as their fingers barely brushed. Static electricity, she gathered, but that unnerved her even more. Her hand retreated, fingers curling back in on themselves to drop to her side.

'Where would you like to start, Mr Romanos?' she asked shakily, refusing to look back up at him again, eager to get moving, to do anything other than be forced to concentrate her eyes on him a second time.

First off, she had collided with dark eyes as impenetrable as black glass and then he had tipped his strong jaw a little as she looked and those eyes had flashed to glittering gold in the sunlight. After that, brain power had kind of receded while he stood there, perfectly at ease and assured, and simply studied her in brooding silence from beneath straight ebony brows and lush black thick lashes. She had worried that she had greeted him wrong or somehow done something he took amiss and nervous tension had almost eaten her alive

'Top floor...obviously,' Aristide told her somewhat drily as he took the lead in heading for the lift, punching the button with an impatient air. 'Tell me about yourself...'

'I'm a temp,' Tabby admitted, hoping that any mistakes she made would be excused on that basis because this male struck her as unlike any accountant she had ever met and she had met a lot while studying and training. 'I work as a PA for Mr Stokes in the sales department—'

'Why am I being welcomed by a temp?' Aristide enquired, watching a flush of colour wash her dainty cheekbones, wondering if she coloured up like that as she came and wholly resolved to find out. It was an instant attraction, he reckoned, an attraction stronger than anything he had felt in quite a few years. He didn't want to recall the last occasion it had happened to him and he blocked off the recollection fast, determined not to revisit that time when he had been young and trusting and really pretty naïve about women and how manipulative they could be when the prize was big enough.

'I don't know, Mr Romanos. I was just asked to come down here. I think it was a request from our CEO—'

'And what's he like?'

'I've never met him,' she said honestly. 'But I think he goes on holiday a lot because he sends photos to my boss...you know the sort of thing. Skiing in the Alps, deep sea diving in the Caribbean, so I assume he's one of those men's men, who like to get physical.'

'As do we all,' Aristide purred, thinking that she could be a mine of information even if it was only common gossip. 'How long have you worked here?'

'Six months. My contract keeps getting renewed, probably because my boss likes me—'

An ebony brow hitched. '*Likes* you?'

Tabby went pink. 'Oh, not like *that*, for goodness' sake! He's a married man with a load of young kids—'

'That doesn't stop a lot of men from straying,' Aristide said with cynical bite. 'My own father was never happier than when he was playing away...'

'Mine too,' Tabby muttered helplessly, quite unsure as to why they should be discussing such things when they had only just met but encouraged by his confidence into giving her own.

Aristide clamped his lips closed, unnerved by how personal he had got with her. He never verged on spilling secrets with his lovers and remained a closed book to all of them. That was a very deliberate policy. He didn't create common ground, he didn't *relax*. But there was something about Tabby, something uniquely warm and inviting and, curiously, she had caught him off guard for a moment.

'Where is everybody?' he asked as they stepped out onto the top floor where he had expected to find the senior staff assembled for his arrival.

'Give me the name of whoever you wish to speak

to and I will get him or her for you. Our finance director is on the floor below,' she told him expectantly.

Aristide had nothing to say to a finance director who hadn't even made it to the top floor in a business that was failing from lack of vigour and direction. 'You can give me a general tour instead,' he told her. 'While you tell me more about yourself.'

Women loved to talk about themselves and rarely realised how much they were revealing in so doing. He had learned that as a child while carefully navigating the stony pathways and fresh rules laid down by every new woman who entered his home. It was second nature for him to explore a woman's background and goals while remaining on the emotional sidelines. All he had to do was plant the occasional encouraging word and he found out about her mother's fragile health, her sister, Violet's bakery and the child her twin was adopting. Clearly they shared very close family ties and he wondered vaguely what that would be like to experience. He heard about how she had gone to university to study accountancy because that had seemed to offer the best hope of a decent career.

'Only I hated it,' Tabby told him.

'Then, why didn't you change your subject?'

'I had already acquired a student loan debt for that year and I didn't want to add to that by dropping out, so I stuck with it and qualified,' Tabby admitted. 'But I think now that I'm working, I should've changed. That's life, isn't it? You don't have a crystal ball to see into the future—'

'Some day you may have your own business and you'll be glad of it then,' Aristide forecast.

Tabitha blinked, not quite sure she wanted to sign up for her own business as she knew her sister worked unbelievably long hours running the bakery. If that was what it would take, she wasn't sure she was ambitious enough to make that jump to greater responsibility. In time, perhaps, but at not yet twenty-two she had ample years ahead in which to create new goals.

Aristide suggested a view of the office space prepared for him. She took him down to the next floor to the empty office right next to the finance director and bustled off to provide him with refreshments. He had no complaint to make about her attitude but she definitely hadn't grasped who he was, he acknowledged. And in a twisty way he kind of enjoyed that ignorance and liked her for not being flirty and all over him as females generally were in his radius. It was oddly refreshing to see the way she looked at him with that warm smile in her eyes that he had never received from a woman before.

But then, he was like all men, he told himself cynically. She was beautiful and he wanted her. Naturally that had to be affecting his judgement. She was sincere and naturally friendly and Aristide was most definitely not accustomed to receiving purely friendly vibes from a woman. Of course, he had immediately wondered if she already had a man in her life, but he also reckoned, with an inner smile, that he would already have heard about such a man if he existed because Tabby didn't keep much to herself.

She just chattered like a stream wending its difficult way through a complex labyrinth but strangely it didn't irritate him, nor did the sudden conversational jumps. He wasn't used to chat with the women he took to bed. He was usually gone too soon after for such frills. Had he been missing out on something? Was it because she was a few years younger than most of the women he met? What was different about her? That lack of visible vanity? That easy laughter? That soothing silence that fell when he hitched a brow and she paused to see what he wanted from her. She was being professional to a superior, not encouragingly submissive.

Out in the tiny kitchenette, Tabby was brewing coffee and her mind was all over the place as though an avalanche had recently engulfed her... *Aristide*. She was totally convinced that she had found the guy she would accomplish that one-night-stand challenge with. He was so beautiful that she had had to force herself to stop staring at him. Her attraction to him was off-the-scale intense and she had never met with that before. He was considerate and interested in her as a person. Perhaps, best of all, he would just be passing through and she wouldn't see him again once his new team of auditors arrived the following day. He had to work for a very large firm because he had mentioned the accident at the airport and if that firm could muster another six employees that fast, they had to be big and important.

'Mr Roma—' she said, flushed from her current thoughts as she walked back into the office carrying a tray.

'Aristide,' he corrected, disconcerting her. 'Will you have dinner with me tonight?'

Her lower lip parted from the upper and she felt his shrewd dark gaze welding to hers, lifting her chin to say, 'I think I would like that—'

Me too, Aristide was tempted to say, watching the tip of her tongue steal out to moisten her full lip, suddenly rigid with sheer lust to a degree that shook him. With her that reaction was instant and he didn't like anything that felt that uncontrolled grabbing a hold of him. It was always *just* sex for him, never anything more, and maybe it was the dreamy deep blue of her eyes that affected him or the softness of her highly feminine face but he still heard himself murmur the warning, 'It will only be one night…'

And to his total surprise, she gave him a huge smile and nodded. 'Perfect,' she told him, while pouring his black coffee and offering him a selection of biscuits, which he ignored. If only all her sex were so practical, he reasoned, while wondering how on earth she could be wholesome one minute and coolly rational and cynical the next. *Perfect?* Women usually wanted and expected a whole lot more from Aristide than one night. In truth, it stung a little that she appeared so content with that likelihood.

He watched her eat three biscuits in succession while he thought about that oddity. In between times she told him about the pervy employee none of the young women would get into a lift with, the executive PA madly in love with her boss and the security guard with the sick wife at the front, who brought her fresh vegetables from his allotment. She gave no names. Even so, she was…indiscreet but warm and entertaining, he decided with a generosity that would have astounded his hospitalised team because he had never tolerated gossip and lighter moments during his working day.

At noon, having seen even the basement service level of the building, Aristide informed Tabby that he had a meeting elsewhere and took his leave of her in the foyer. 'If you give me your address I'll pick you up tonight at eight,' he murmured lightly.

And she did, stumbling a little over the syllables, far more excited by the idea of a date than she felt she ought to be. After all, no one knew better than her how untrustworthy men could be. Of course, she had met exceptions to that rule, hadn't allowed her father's cruelties to turn her into a man-hater. She did have occasional dates, although none had amounted to much because she had never been attracted enough to get closer to a guy or to take that risk on catching feelings that weren't even wanted.

But the knowledge that she was to marry a stranger in six weeks and do without socialising or having sex if *she* wanted sex was a restriction her pride and self-respect could not accept. This night with Aristide would be *her* choice, her chance to assert her rights over her own body while she still could. There was no way she was running the risk that her stranger husband might be expecting bed privileges into the bargain and that he would then become her *first* lover. No, that little detail would be taken care of off stage and prior to that stupid marriage when nobody would even know about it.

And then, if her mother required some very expensive further treatment to continue her life, as the wife of the wealthy Tore Renzetti, she would be easily able to afford to cover the costs. Why else would she continue agreeing to the marriage after their grandfather had virtually refused to pay up for his daughter's care? With the number of health crises their mother had suffered in recent years, Tabby knew that she had to be aware of the risk that more might lie ahead.

Tabby adored her mother, even if she hadn't always been a mother she could respect as a woman. Lucia Blessington was a very caring, compassionate person and endlessly supportive of her twin girls. Even though her daughters had had a very unhappy childhood while their father was still around, Tabby and Violet had forgiven Lucia for giving their horrible father too many chances to reform.

Now that their parents were divorced and they had no further contact with Sam Blessington, their lives had become calm and peaceful. Now there was no man coming home in a drunken rage and lashing out with his fists or frittering away their mother's earnings. Now Violet and Tabby between them could look forward to keeping their mother out of those low-paid jobs that had been all she was able to get while they were still children.

'Julian's flying back early from his break in Cuba,' Ed informed Tabby worriedly when she returned after lunch. 'He told me that Traxis has been taken over. We'll just have to hope that it's not to one of those asset-strippers, keen to throw us all out of work and sell the building!'

Tabby got back to the flat she shared with several other girls that evening and went straight to her room to trail out her wardrobe and decide what to wear. But it wasn't *really* a date, she reminded herself. He had been quite clear about what it would be and she was fine with that, wasn't she?

The stirring of unease within her warned her that she was less confident than she would have liked about her decision. After all, here she was heading for twenty-two years of age and no *right* male had come along. She hadn't fallen in love and contrived to share a bed in the more natural way. She hadn't even been insanely attracted to a guy until that very same day. So, Aristide was simply the best available option. That was all the evening would be.

It would be like a date, Aristide was thinking with a frown while he showered. And he didn't *do* dates. What was it about Tabitha Blessington that knocked him off balance? As a rule, he met women at events, in businesses or through friends. He didn't ask them out anyplace, he just took them home, whether that be to a hotel or one of his properties. Dinner engagements didn't enter the proceedings. But he had had the suspicion that she would say no if he framed his desire any more frankly. And he hadn't wanted that. No, he hadn't wanted that at all. *Thee mou*, when had he last been this worked up about being with a woman? It was nonsensical and out of character.

By the time the door buzzer went, Tabby was dressed and ready, clad in a casual blue mini dress and a pair of high heels. She hadn't bothered with make-up. After all, it wasn't some romantic date, she reminded herself, opening the door to a middle-aged stranger.

'Mr Romanos is waiting in the car for you, Miss Blessington.'

Romanos, *that* was his name. She hadn't quite caught it when she'd first met him and then hadn't liked to ask him to repeat it lest he think she was pretty incompetent. 'And you are?' she queried quietly.

'His driver…'

Tabby followed the older man down the stairs, her brow furrowed. His *driver*? Who had a driver in London where most travelled by public transport? Only very well-off people. Possibly he was a director in the accountancy firm, she reasoned uncertainly.

She was extremely rattled to find the door of a silver limousine falling open for her arrival. Aristide folded out to his full height and gave her a slashing smile. In that moment, he looked so heart-stoppingly handsome and charismatic that her mouth ran dry and her wits might as well have been dandelion clocks floating in the breeze.

'You look amazing,' he murmured huskily, ushering her into the limo while his driver hovered, openly disconcerted by his employer's presence on the pavement.

No regrets about making the dinner date, Aristide was already thinking as he sank in beside her. The blue of her eyes matched the dress or maybe the blue of the dress heightened the colour of her eyes. He blinked, wondering why he was abstracted enough to think such a thing while simultaneously acknowledging that she was even more beautiful than he remembered her being only hours earlier, pale hair like rumpled silk lying across her narrow shoulders, a heart-shaped silver locket at her delicate collarbone. Somehow his brain conjured up an image of sapphires there instead.

'So, it seems that I've misunderstood who you are somewhere along the way,' Tabby remarked stiffly, intimidated by the level of opulence in the big vehicle. 'I believed that you worked for Millwrights—'

'No, I own Millwrights. They run audits for me,' Aristide told her casually. 'I did wonder what was happening this morning when nobody appeared for my benefit, but your charming company was a plus and I let it go.'

Tabby breathed in deep and slow, steadying her

nerves. 'Then may I ask why you were at Traxis today?'

'I bought it over—'

'Traxis?' Tabby gasped in surprise and consternation because it was an international company. 'You *own* it?'

Good heavens, had she allowed herself to be chatted up by her new employer?

'If you're my boss, I shouldn't be here with you!' Tabby exclaimed in dismay. 'If you stop the car, I'll get out here—'

Aristide studied her in wonderment. 'Are you mad? I'm not your boss. I won't be taking much of an active part in running Traxis. My role is behind the scenes. I buy companies, reorganise them and then move on to the next,' he explained levelly.

Her heart still beating very fast at the belief that she was not only way out of her depth with such a guy but also doing something wrong in going out with him, Tabby stared back at him anxiously. 'I'm still not sure I should be with you—'

A big lean brown hand closed over hers where she had braced her own on the seat. 'Relax, *angelos mou*,' he urged. 'Of course you should be with me tonight. It's what you want…and what I want. Why should anything else come into it?'

CHAPTER TWO

'It's what you want...and what I want.'

That was the indisputable truth, Tabby conceded. But Aristide made it sound so simple, although wasn't it simple? she asked herself. Two young people surrendering to an attraction and getting together, two people unlikely, it seemed, to meet again. It was just he wasn't the more ordinary salaried guy she had assumed he was, no, he was evidently quite wealthy. But ought she to hold that difference against him? My goodness, Violet would enjoy this story...

Only as soon as Tabby thought that, she reddened, knowing that there was no way she would be sharing this particular story with her sister. She suspected that her twin would be a little shocked by what she was about to do, not judgemental, of course, but definitely surprised. It was more likely a tale she would tell somewhere down the road after this fake-marriage nonsense was behind her and life had returned to normal.

Aristide was still holding her hand, she registered,

and she liked that, liked that quiet connection so much that it was a disappointment when he freed her fingers and the limo stopped and it was clear that they were about to leave the car.

A faint darker line of colour scored Aristide's cheekbones as he curved a guiding hand to her slender back on the way into the exclusive restaurant. Once again he was wondering what was wrong with him because it was a challenge to keep his hands off her, even in a non-sexual way. What was that about? Maybe he would find out what she was doing over the weekend, extend their future. No, he told himself harshly, that would be getting into relationship territory and he wasn't going in that direction *ever again*.

As they were greeted at the door like important people and led through the packed tables, her companion acknowledging several comments, Tabby felt severely underdressed for the first time in her life. Her little cotton sundress didn't cut the mustard amongst company that wore glittering jewels and cocktail-type frocks. Cheeks warm, she sank down at the secluded table, grateful they weren't in the centre of the dining room where she had already spotted a couple of famous television actors.

Aristide could read her expressive face as easily as a book. The surroundings intimidated her and he should've put more thought into their location. Since he hadn't, he endeavoured to tease and entertain her while she perused the menu. Before very long, her easy smile was back and she was laughing.

He couldn't take his attention off her and it felt too intense for him and a shard of uneasiness pierced him afresh. He didn't want to be involved, he didn't want to *get* involved and he was handing out the wrong signals, wasn't he? One night or even two was his limit and he didn't wish to mislead her. Striving to cool his attitude, he became quieter.

Tabby was mesmerised by Aristide, the ease of his manners, the witty edge to his conversation, the way his attention never once strayed from her even though there were two very beautiful, well-dressed women at a nearby table. And when it was time to leave and she only then thought of what lay ahead, she found herself getting nervous and quieter as well.

She knew that she could say that she wanted to go home and Aristide was unlikely to say anything, she reckoned. He had been way too kind to her to suddenly turn nasty, she reasoned. The only problem was that she didn't *want* to leave Aristide behind, didn't want to backtrack and never know what it would be like to *be* with him. And that seemed to be telling her that, for her, he was the right guy.

'Where are we going?' she asked uncertainly as the limo drove off again.

'To my home here. It's an apartment,' Aristide imparted, releasing his belt and leaning closer. 'I'm not sure that I can contain myself that long. I want to kiss you—'

A faint scent of cologne assailed her nostrils, reminding her of icy forest nights and, beneath it, the aroma of clean, husky male. He smelled so good she wanted to bottle him and sniff that scent like an addict. 'Go ahead,' she framed raggedly, meeting eyes like dark beaten gold in the lights flickering through the tinted windows of the dark streets outside.

His mouth closed over hers and she was electrified from that first moment. It was that connection she had sought and waited for and never found. Her heart was beating so fast it seemed to be in her ears. He kissed her breathless, his tongue delving deep, teaching her other longings, other needs, spurring a building tightness between her slender thighs.

'We're here...'

Aristide was, once again, unsettled as he had forgotten where they were. He climbed out, hugely aroused, struggling not to recall that the last time he had kissed anyone like that, he had been about sixteen or so. And his first thought, a kneejerk reaction, was 'send her home'. It was followed by the awareness that there was no way he could do that without discovering what it was about Tabby Blessington that sent him into a tailspin. He would find out that it was simply a stronger than usual case of sexual attraction, he told himself soothingly.

'My goodness, how long were we doing that for?' Tabby mumbled as he ushered her into the lift.

'I don't care,' Aristide admitted, reaching for her again to cover her kiss-swollen lips with his own.

Feeling his lean, powerful physique sealed to hers unleashed another whole set of effects in Tabby. He virtually carried her through a door into the apartment and she was blind and mute, seeing nothing, saying nothing, only wanting the taste of him back on her lips and the feel of him against her.

Aristide scooped her up into his arms and carried her down to his bedroom. They had finally got there and he could hardly hold his libido back. Never had he felt such impatience, such eagerness.

Tabby surfaced from that mindlessness that had gripped her from the instant he'd touched her and gazed at him with concealed wonder. She was feeling what she had always dreamt of feeling, physically and emotionally and, even though she had told herself that there was nothing emotional about what she was about to do, she ignored that self-warning.

Aristide cast off his jacket, yanked at his tie, kicked off his shoes. He was struggling to hold back, to pace himself, stay in control. 'I find you incredibly attractive,' he confided in a driven undertone.

Tabby followed his lead more awkwardly and slid off her heels, pausing, not quite sure whether she should be stripping, which she was a little too shy to do for the first time with a man. Should she be waiting for him to undress her?

He came back to her and kissed her again and she felt his hands at her shoulders. Taking courage, she stepped back and lifted the dress off over her head, which was the only way to remove it, leaving herself bare but for her bra and panties. He pulled her back to him and then she remembered the one thing she had sworn she would never forget, and she pulled free to run back and grab her little envelope purse and dig into it for the item there she had been carrying round for just such a purpose for years. Cheeks scarlet, she pressed it into his hand and said shakily, 'Use this…'

A woman had never in Aristide's entire existence handed him protection to use before because he always used his own. It was a weird request, he thought, but everyone had their quirks and possibly this was hers. He tossed the condom down on the bed and embarked on unbuttoning his shirt. His hands weren't quite steady because any kind of control when she set him on fire was a challenge.

He hadn't argued and Tabby was hugely relieved but, ever since being warned that there was an occasional man who damaged protection because his private kink was 'breeding' from a woman or because he was keen to pass on some unmentionable disease, she had been determined that such a thing would never happen to her. Not that she thought Aristide was of that ilk, yet how could anyone know such a thing if only one night was to be shared? Better safe than sorry, she reflected, glad that that moment of embarrassment was already past.

The shirt dropped to the floor and revealed Aristide's breathtakingly male physique. Her admiring eyes roamed over prominent pecs, an indented torso, strong biceps and the legendary V muscles disappearing below the waistband of his trousers. He was so beautiful, top-to-toe beautiful like a pin-up, and she marvelled that she had never before seen a male in that light.

Aristide surveyed her slender frame with fierce hunger roaring through him. She was sort of hovering beside the bed, giving him the vibe that she hadn't as much experience as he might have thought, but that was no deal-breaker for Aristide, who had once fallen intensely in love with a woman simply because he'd believed that she had chosen him to be her first lover. The treacherous betrayal that had followed a few years afterwards still bit deep.

Ever since then, the concept of virginity had turned him off. It was a social construct, an out-of-date expectation that had once wowed his ancestors, not something he would ever seek on his own behalf. It certainly didn't mean that that virgin would magically be pure of heart and faithful.

'You seem nervous,' Aristide commented as he closed his arms round her again, still finding it difficult to disconnect from a need to touch her continually. More than just lust, more than he would allow himself to *feel*, he finally recognised. He would handle it, of course he would, by being sensible, by walking away afterwards as he always did.

A tight smile curved her lush pretty mouth. 'I haven't done this much,' she muttered apologetically.

For the first time in his life, Aristide wished he could've said the same and as soon as that bizarre thought occurred to him, he shut it down fast, tugging her into his arms and kissing her, before lifting her and bringing her down on his bed.

'I want you so much, *angelos mou*,' he husked, detaching her bra with a skilled hand.

'Me too,' she managed unevenly, stretching up to taste his mouth again, already addicted. 'What language is that?'

'I'm Greek, born and bred.' Aristide was distracted by the small, pretty breasts he had unveiled, dipping his head to catch the hard little button of a pink nipple between his lips and dally there.

Tabby writhed, that first touch more than enough to set fire in her already overheated body. Long fingers tugged at the peaks of her sensitive breasts and her hips rose, catching her breath suddenly a challenge, her heart racing. And then he traced the heart of her, scoring the tender flesh still shielded by her panties, setting a flickering flame to the tingling nerve endings there.

'I need to be inside you,' Aristide groaned half under his breath, wildly impatient as he could never remember being before. He skimmed off her last garment, exploring the delicate damp flesh, teasing her clit and inserting a finger. By then, she was gasping, twisting and turning under the onslaught of more delightful sensation than she had ever dreamt would feature in her first experience.

And then he was reaching for protection, tearing it open with his teeth, leaning back from her to use it and she really could not help seeing that there was rather more of him than she had expected. She tensed, bracing herself even though she knew she should relax, and then he was sliding over her, lifting her up to him and her whole body was screaming with impatience for his next move even though she was nervous.

He eased into her slowly, with more care than she could have hoped to receive, but still it burned a little, stung as that part of her stretched to accommodate his invasion.

'*Thee mou*...you're so tight.'

As he lifted her to him, he plunged his hips and a stark jolt of pain raced through her, disconcerting her, startling her, and she gave a little gasp between clenched teeth, thinking that *that* had hurt more than she had been prepared for. She tucked the knowledge away fast, fighting to get back into the moment and still savour the other feelings.

Like being so close, so connected to him and she liked that. And the worst was over, past, she reckoned, a truth proven by the reawakening of those sensitive sensations at her core as he shifted position and with one ruthless twist of his agile hips sent a current of pure pleasure shooting through her whole being. Brilliant dark golden eyes assailed hers in a collision she felt to her very marrow. Her heart pounded and then he was moving. Sensation raced through her in ever surging waves until she was straining frantically to reach some distant peak of perfection.

But before she could reach that peak, he eased off

her and flipped her over to change position. A little whimper of complaint escaped her because she would have dragged him back by force had he dared to walk off at that point. Every fibre of her was pleading for that ultimate end goal. He drove into her again. Hard. Deep. She was struggling to catch her breath, her heart banging so hard she was afraid it would burst and then suddenly it was happening for her, every sensation merging into a wondrous whole that blew her away. Fireworks detonated low in her belly and blissful pleasure washed through every nerve cell. Shaken by everything she had felt, she felt him reach completion as well.

She slumped down on the bed and then slowly eased round onto her back again.

Aristide vaulted off the bed in a rage. The condom had split, the condom *she* had insisted he use. He snatched up the discarded wrapper and checked the expiration date with a vocal growl of disbelief. 'You *gave* me an expired condom to use! What sort of a scam is this?'

In shock at the angry words, Tabby emerged from her stupor, suddenly feeling very naked and exposed. She slid off the bed to grab up her dress, putting it on over her head fast to feel covered again. Covered, the way you wanted to be when under attack. And that was how she felt: under *attack* at the least likely moment, when she was completely unprepared for the development.

'*Expired?*' she repeated chokily as he tossed the

wrapper down on the bed between them rather as an official would produce Exhibit A in a courtroom. She lifted it and saw that he was correct from the date stamp. How long had she carried that item in her purse? Evidently longer than she should've done and she was only now recalling that she had invested in that box while she was at university. 'I'm sorry... I should've checked,' she muttered awkwardly, discreetly retrieving her bra and panties, digging the first into her bag and sliding into the second because she refused to travel home bare beneath her dress.

'And on top of that, you were a virgin too, weren't you?' Aristide prompted tautly.

Tabby paled. 'I don't think that has any relevance here but, for the sake of clarity...yes, I was.'

'I don't aspire to sleep with virgins,' Aristide informed her with scorn. 'And between the expired protection and your virginity, you've pretty much got the market covered when it comes to suspicious circumstances.' He studied her with hard dark accusing eyes as if they had not been as intimate as two people could be only minutes earlier.

His attitude in the aftermath of that intimacy was like a slap in the face, only she suspected it hurt more than the slap would've done. 'I didn't realise,' she said with determined dignity, 'that being a virgin was a hanging offence.'

'You could've told me. A normal woman would've warned me but you chose not to and that silence, combined with the expired safeguard, would make any man doubtful of your motivation!' he condemned angrily.

Tabby raised a dark blonde brow. 'I'm afraid I can't imagine what possible motivation I could've had other than the obvious...having sex with you,' she completed coldly, getting her armour on now, beginning to recover from her rude awakening to his opinion of her.

'You're not that naïve, nobody is, not these days!' he shot back at her. 'I'm a very wealthy man and I refuse to be a target for women who wish to enrich themselves at my expense—'

Tabby's rarely roused temper flared up in white-hot flames of fire inside her chest because she had had more than enough of his toxic assumptions about her character. 'Oh, if that's what you're worried about, I can free you of your fear,' she assured him almost sweetly. 'I'm getting married in seven weeks to a man who's... I assume...just as rich as you. I don't need to trade my virginity like a commodity, Mr Romanos, or run the risk of pregnancy to entrap any man. Rather an old-fashioned accusation that, don't you think? In fact if the contraceptive mishap *were* to result in consequences, I'd be the one in a serious fix!'

Aristide listened in growing disbelief. He couldn't believe what he was hearing! She was getting married, she was engaged to marry some other man in a few weeks and yet she had let *him* take her to bed? None of that made sense to him. If she was engaged, why had she still been untouched? He was shocked, appalled, and he was so angry as he pulled on clothes that he was shaking with the force of his emotions.

'So, you're a cheat as well as everything else,' he breathed tightly.

'Goodnight, Mr Romanos. Can't say it's been nice because, like other men I've met, you're not quite what you seem to be on the surface,' Tabby fired back at him with hot cheeks and a strong desire to push him fully clothed into the nearest weed-clogged pond.

'I'll take you home...' Aristide addressed her rigidly turned back as she reached the front door.

'No, thanks.' And with that calm retort, Tabby walked out of his penthouse apartment and finally felt able to breathe again.

'Tabitha...'

She turned her tousled head and arrowed glacial blue eyes back at him as she awaited the lift.

'If there *should* be consequences—'

'Forget it,' Tabitha murmured pleasantly. 'I wouldn't come begging to you if I was down to my very last penny and *starving*. That's a promise.'

Aristide strode back indoors and closed the door quietly when he wanted to slam it. What the hell was Tabby Blessington playing at? Well, he intended to find out. Pulling out his phone, he texted her name and address to the private investigation agency he used and requested a full report on her. He was angry, frustrated and, yes, there was dissatisfaction too at the manner in which he had discovered her true nature. She had cheated on her fiancé with him. Acknowledging that reality, he told himself that he should be grateful to be made so swiftly aware of her capacity for deceit.

Tabby travelled home on the Tube, had a shower and went straight to bed. She longed to phone her twin and tell her what had happened but she cringed at the image of her having made an outsize fool of herself. There she had been, all sentimental and romantic about Aristide Romanos in spite of the fact it was only meant to be a one-night stand. No, she decided, she would take those short-lived girlie dreams to the grave with her. She had *asked* to be hurt, she told herself with self-loathing, she had turned out to be much more vulnerable than she had ever believed herself to be.

And why, when he had insinuated that she was after him for his money, had she responded with the news that she was due to marry another rich man in seven weeks? Why hadn't she foreseen that he would naturally assume that she was a faithless cheater into the bargain? He hadn't wanted to be her first lover either. There was something insulting about that, but it would be perfectly understandable if he simply preferred more experienced partners. And she had naïvely supposed that he wouldn't notice her innocence!

No, Aristide had been a disaster, but at least she had accomplished her goal. She squirmed in her bed, still aching, telling herself it served her right. She would probably confess all to Violet in a few months, once the crushing humiliation of her encounter with Aristide had faded a bit.

And the condom had let them both down. She had to worry about that as well, she reminded herself. But she brushed off that concern because she literally could not even begin to imagine being pregnant. Why borrow trouble when she was in a big enough mess as it was with a stranger bridegroom-to-be to meet at the altar in only seven weeks' time?

CHAPTER THREE

Turning full circle back from those memories and returning to the present, Tabby stared down at that positive pregnancy test and tossed it in the bin. The deed was done, the wondering at an end and full reality had set in.

That very same morning she had had an appointment with her future husband's lawyers to sign the pre-nup. She had forged her sister's signature in Violet's usual scrawl and shame covered her from head to toe because she had let her twin down badly. She was the single one of the two of them, free of dependants and a business, and naturally it would have been easier for her to make that commercial alliance. Now Violet, with the baby daughter she was adopting and a very demanding bakery, was about to be thrown in at the deep end to marry Tore Renzetti instead and, of course, Tabby felt terrible about that. Her unfortunate sister would be forced to make many more compromises than would have been demanded of Tabby, whose life had been more fluid and free of responsibility.

Tabby followed that act up with a visit to her twin, needing to confess her sins as soon as possible. She greeted her twin's childminder, Joy, who was also Violet's tenant, who told her that her niece, Belle, was down for a nap, having eaten. Tabby told Joy that she could leave early, leaving Tabby free to pace the floor in the tiny lounge.

Before Violet had even adjusted to her unannounced visit, Tabby had to dart off to the bathroom in haste where she was sick, an ever increasing reminder of her condition, she reflected unhappily.

'It's not a bug,' Tabby revealed tautly when she reappeared, her lovely face troubled and embarrassed. 'I wouldn't be visiting if I had anything contagious. No, the truth is that I'm pregnant.'

'Pregnant?' Violet gasped in disbelief. 'But *how*? I mean—'

'Not a virgin any more,' Tabby cut in somewhat bitterly. 'You have to remember me saying that there was no way I was going into this marriage a virgin and staying that way for another three years!'

'So, if you're pregnant, who's the father?' Violet asked worriedly.

Tabby grimaced. 'Someone I met at work who I believed was just passing through. I thought he would be perfect as I'd never see him again but the birth control let me down.'

Her twin studied her with sympathy. 'What are you going to do?'

'It's more a question of what *you* are going to do,' Tabitha stated, turning the question back on her sister. 'After all, I can't marry Tore Renzetti now that I'm pregnant. It would be a breach of the contract I signed and I can't hide it, so I'll have to 'fess up and then the marriage won't go ahead and that means we don't get the money upfront to cover Mum's clinical trial.'

Like Tabby, Violet was horrified by that idea because everything they had agreed had been for their mother's benefit to enable the older woman to get further treatment unavailable in the UK.

'I've already committed you,' Tabby admitted with a grimace of apology. 'I signed the pre-nup in your name. We can't take the risk at this stage that Renzetti will back out—'

'But *would* he? He must want those shares pretty badly to agree to this in the first place. And how am I supposed to pretend to be you when I'm six inches shorter and as dark-haired as you're fair? His legal team *has* seen you,' Violet reminded her in dismay.

'For the wedding, we'll stick you in high heels and a blonde wig with a veil on top. We can swing it if we try hard enough,' Tabby declared with characteristic fortitude.

The worst of her challenges accomplished, Violet's forgiveness for the bride swap freely given and gratefully accepted, Tabby returned to her shared flat. Her sister had already suggested that she move in with her because her tenant, Joy, was moving out. And Tabby could then easily take over running the bakery when Violet was absent.

The offer had only reminded Tabby that she had no permanent employment, no security. Not a good place to be in with a child on the way, she acknowledged, but she didn't want to be a burden on Violet, who had quite enough on her plate now with that horrid marriage ahead of her in less than two weeks. Three years at the mercy of some guy who neither of them knew a thing about. He was very good-looking too, likely slick and a womaniser, Tabby assumed, having already done her social media exploration on the father of her child.

There was nothing good to be found out about Aristide Romanos online. He was never seen with the same woman twice which said it all, she thought grimly. Surely only a rampant playboy would be worrying about a virgin scamming him with a faulty contraceptive? Or had some unsavoury event turned Aristide bitter and suspicious? It was a struggle but she was trying to be fair, trying not to hate and demonise the guy who had turned a single wild night, as it were, into a mere hour of humiliation. She wouldn't forgive him for that in a hurry, even if he *was* going to be the father of her child. She didn't care how rich and successful he was. That wasn't an excuse.

At work several weeks later, she received a call back from the doctor's surgery for another visit and groaned out loud. Being pregnant certainly seemed to run up the medical attention she required, although if they were able to give her something to combat the terrible nausea with which she was already suffering she would decide to be grateful. Now that she had taken over managing the bakery, she was surrounded by the fumes of food all day and it exacerbated the morning sickness.

That same evening, feeling like death warmed over, she was on her way out to keep her medical appointment when she walked out of the door of the flat and was confronted by the sight of Aristide in the flesh at the top of the stairs. 'Oh!' she gasped in panic, taken aback by the disconcerting sight of him when she had never expected to see him again.

'Tabby…' he positively purred, the benevolent tone ill matched to the slanting tension of the smile he dared to accompany it.

'What the heck are you doing here?' Tabby demanded sharply, in no mood to pretend that he could ever be a welcome visitor. 'I don't want to see you… I don't want to speak to you either!'

'Whatever else I may be, I'm responsible,' Aristide informed her, falling behind her as she clattered on downstairs, ignoring him. 'Obviously I need to speak to you again to address what happened between us last month.'

Although, in truth, Aristide was thinking that he probably wouldn't have bothered had it been any other woman in the starring role. But this was Tabby,

Tabby the curiosity, whom he still couldn't get out of his mind, even if it was very possible that she was a gold-digger. How did he know? How could he even find out without seeing her again? So, it *was* a case of acting responsibly, he assured himself.

'Not as I see it,' Tabby said breathlessly as she headed down the next flight of stairs.

'I need to know if you're all right,' Aristide bit out impatiently.

All right? Being sick all the time and tired every hour of the day was all right?

'No, I'm *not* all right!' Tabby snapped back without thought or any more patience than he had. 'I'm pregnant and that is definitely not all right with me!'

Aristide was stunned, frozen to the spot as she disappeared ahead of him. By the time he reached street level there was no sign of her and frustration swelled inside him, threatening to overflow like a tidal wave. How could she just drop *that* on him and then disappear without another word? What sort of woman was she?

A young woman of twenty-one without anyone to fall back on for support, his sane mind recalled. He now knew almost everything there was to know about Tabby Blessington. He didn't know the details of the planned marriage she had flung in his teeth two months earlier but, more importantly, he knew that the wedding had gone ahead *without* her as the bride. He was also aware that she had quit her job as a temp and was in the process of moving out of her current accommodation into her sister's apartment above the bakery, which she was currently running.

Tabby submitted to another blood test at the health centre with poor grace. The nurse mentioned the need for her to make another doctor's appointment to see if anything could be done to help her with the morning sickness. Tabby made that appointment at the desk but she was really running on automatic pilot because everything after Aristide's appearance had taken on the oddest sense of unreality.

Aristide, standing there as if he had stepped out of a dream, looking exactly the same as he had looked that day they first met. Ridiculously tall, impossibly handsome, black hair a little ruffled and long enough to start curling, something she suspected he usually curbed by keeping it shorter. Nothing had changed for him but *everything* had changed for her. And it would've been a lie to deny that she was somewhat bitter and resentful over the truth that a woman suffered more than a man when she fell pregnant. A glimpse of Aristide, untouched by all the chaos that had engulfed her, had infuriated her and betrayed her into an honesty she would never have given him in any other circumstances. So, now that he knew there had been *consequences*, she wouldn't see him for dust, she assumed with satisfaction.

Aristide was in shock and grateful not to be in the middle of his working day. Tabby's fertility and his own had run a coach and horses through his life plan. Life had a habit of wrecking such ideas with the unexpected, he reasoned, straightening his spine. A baby…there was going to be a baby. But the minute he thought that, he realised that he didn't know even that for a fact. She might not be planning to go ahead and actually have the baby. He could not afford to make such an assumption when on that score the future was hers to choose. Sobered by that reflection, Aristide poured another strong drink and he sat down to consider matters he had once hoped to *never* have to consider again. He also reached conclusions that shook him rigid and contributed to another sleepless night.

The next morning, Tabby arrived at the bakery in a rideshare with her cases, reaching them out as fast as she could, toting them one by one across the pavement. She stowed them inside the street door of Violet's apartment upstairs and went into the bakery next door to start her working day. She had taken over the running of the bakery for her sister's benefit. She couldn't do the baking, for which Luca, an Italian pastry chef, had been hired, but she could handle the shop, the staff and the payroll.

In the tiny closet of an office space, Tabby checked the rotas, dealt with a salary query and made notes on the daily special orders for Luca's benefit.

'When I have my break at eleven, you'll join me for coffee,' Luca declared with warm dark eyes resting on hers.

'Whatever…' Tabby was weary of fighting off the Italian's come-ons, past caring if he forced her to the stage of saying an outright no. If he took offence, on her head be it even though the bakery couldn't function without his skills. Did he truly fancy her or was he merely under the impression that a female manager had to be convinced that he did? She couldn't believe his attraction to her was real when she knew that she was looking less than her best with pasty skin and dark circles below her eyes. And even her hair was going awry while her hormones seemed to be going into overdrive with her pregnancy.

Later, Luca snared her from behind the counter to share morning coffee with him and Tabby was trying to head him off at the pass, as it were, before she decided to simply be honest. 'Luca, I've just discovered that I'm pregnant,' she admitted awkwardly. 'So, really this is a case of bad timing—'

'Is the father with you?' Luca enquired with startling immediacy.

'Er, no,' she muttered with a grimace.

'Then we can be friends, if nothing else,' Luca told her with the easy English he had acquired while working in New York for several years, his dark eyes continuing to gleam with warmth and acceptance as he laid his hand down on hers in a soothing gesture.

And a friend worked for Tabby at that moment as nothing else could have done because, as well as Luca being very easy on the eye, Tabby had no friends in whom she had confided her secret. Why? The majority of her uni pals would have suggested a termination for an inconvenient, uncommitted pregnancy and that wasn't what she wanted, so she would've been out of step with them.

Aristide strode into the bakery with his bodyguards in tow like an invading Viking horde and froze in his path when he paused to take in the sight of the *mother* of his child having her hand fondled by another man, clad in chef whites. For a split second, he hovered in an uncharacteristic act of hesitation.

Tabby saw him straight away. Really, there was no chance of *not* noticing Aristide, the sheer height of him in a fancy dark suit, his gorgeous dark curly head held high, his keen dark golden eyes scanning the shop while the couple of males accompanying him fell back to the wall to watch him. Whoa, Aristide had a security team, she registered, wondering where they had been the day he visited Traxis.

'Excuse me,' she said to Luca as she rose from her seat. 'I'll see you later.'

Tabby stalked over to Aristide, attitude in every stressed line of her small, slender frame. 'What are you doing here?'

'Are you serious?' Aristide enquired in disbelief at that greeting. 'We need to talk.'

Tabby thought through several incendiary replies and discarded them because she already knew that Aristide was stubborn, impatient and possibly even a little dramatic. She didn't need him or any of that in her life but she hadn't yet contrived to tell him that, so she could accept that, after her announcement that she was expecting his child, a further conversation had to be had. 'Yes,' she conceded, feeling generous. 'But right now, I'm working—'

'You're the manager,' he reminded her and she wondered how he knew that.

'But this is a very busy shop and if I take time out to talk to you, something may come up,' she pointed out while thinking, to her annoyance, that he had the most breathtakingly beautiful eyes of anyone she had ever met, liquid gold like a burnished sunset and surprisingly eloquent even when he wasn't speaking. She sensed his urgency even though he had said nothing to express the feeling and it changed her mind.

Spinning round, she told the bakery's senior sales assistant that she was in charge until Tabby's return and, escorting Aristide back out onto the street, she unlocked her new front door again, apologising for the cases in their path.

'You shouldn't be lifting anything heavy up a staircase,' Aristide told her unnecessarily, because she was already painfully aware of all the shoulds and shouldn'ts in her immediate pregnant future.

'Are you going to take care of my luggage?' she asked snarkily.

'No, but my employees will,' Aristide asserted smoothly.

'Didn't think you'd be doing it,' Tabby commented snidely.

'I'm not ashamed that I pay others to take care of the necessities of life,' Aristide countered. 'My talents lie in other fields.'

'Not with the right word at the right time, if my experience of you can bear witness,' Tabby told him tightly.

'What transpired between us is entirely another story,' Aristide replied with a hint of defensiveness, sufficient to compress her lips on further provocative remarks. After all, she had nothing to gain from arguing with Aristide, indeed it might even convince him to stay longer and she didn't want that to happen.

Upstairs, she showed him into the tiny sitting room, smiling with relief when her cases were piled at the door, one after another.

'Where's your bedroom?' Aristide asked suddenly. 'I'll move them there.'

'The room at the end of the corridor,' she supplied while thinking that she would be occupying her sister's bedroom, sleeping in *her* bed with *her* sheets and that nothing around her actually *belonged* to her. Now that her sister was married, she no longer had much use for the apartment.

For the first time that was a rather deflating acknowledgement of the truth that, in getting pregnant and losing her independence, she had kind of become her twin's dependant. She reddened, knowing her sister would argue with such a statement but feeling it all the same as she was the elder twin, the one who had been born first, the one who liked to think she was the leading, protective half of the pair. Only not any more...

Tabby was shaken to appreciate, when she

emerged from those pointless thoughts, that Aristide had moved her luggage down to the bedroom all by *himself*. It struck her that he was on his very best behaviour and that she would be rude if she offered him less. 'Would you like coffee?' she asked him as he reappeared, annoyingly looking not the least creased or out of breath from that physical effort.

'No, thank you,' he breathed, striding the small distance to the window, turning at the sight of the heavy traffic on the road outside and facing her again, dark eyes narrowed. 'I need to ask you, but it may not suit you to respond right now. Are you planning to have this child?'

Shame engulfed Tabby in a heated surge and she coloured. It hadn't occurred to her to think that he might be interested in asking such a very basic question. And yet it was an obvious question in today's world. Aristide had more layers than she had allowed him to have in her imagination, where she had demonised him. 'Yes. I will be having the baby,' she told him rather woodenly because, ironically, it felt like a very personal question from him that she didn't really want to answer even though common sense was warning her that it would be his baby as well.

Unexpectedly, Aristide appeared to relax at that admission and he smiled, moved to the armchair beside him and folded his big athletic frame down. 'Then, if it's not too late to change my mind, I would like coffee—'

Feeling a little dizzy at the surprise of that smile

on such a subject, Tabby ducked into the kitchenette and then winced as the cupboard came up empty on the coffee that her twin rarely drank. 'There's no coffee…' she muttered in the doorway.

Aristide shrugged a wide, strong shoulder. 'I was only trying to be polite—'

'Is it that much of an effort for you with me?' she sliced in, unable to still the words on her tongue before she voiced them and then suddenly raising both hands. 'Forget I said that! Possibly I'm in a hostile mood—'

'Understandably. I assume this development has changed your life a huge amount because you didn't marry Tore Renzetti,' Aristide stated, disconcerting her with the sheer level of his knowledge about her.

'You've had me investigated…or something,' she muttered without surprise, reckoning that such caution and precision went with his sharp-edged, ruthless personality.

'Guilty as charged. I had to know what was going on and I'm afraid I still don't understand that relationship,' Aristide declared.

'It was supposed to be a business alliance. I'm not sorry to have missed out on marrying the guy—I mean, I never met him—but I'm *very* sorry and guilty that my sister had to marry him instead.'

'None of my business,' Aristide forced himself to say when really he wanted every tiny detail of that arrangement because he had an overriding need to know everything about her. However, he had heard enough to know that the heir to Renzetti Pharma would not be hovering on the sidelines of Tabby's life even though he had married another woman. Truly, that was the only angle, the sole possibility, that had still concerned him. If she had never met the man, there was no relationship to be considered. And if the sister had got him instead, that was even better.

'I really don't understand what you're doing here. I'm newly pregnant,' she pointed out uncomfortably. 'Now that you know I'm going to have this baby, you can—'

'I want to take you to see a good obstetrician and have you fully checked over,' Aristide announced without hesitation. 'It will be a private appointment in hospital. You are not obliged to agree to the idea but I would be grateful if you did.'

'Why do you want to take me to see a doctor?' Tabby was astonished by the suggestion.

'According to one of my cousins, pregnant women glow,' Aristide murmured wryly. 'You're still beautiful but you're not glowing.'

'I'd forgotten how charming you could be...saying all that instead of just biting the bullet and telling me the truth that I look like hell right now!'

'It's not like that—'

'It's exactly like that,' she interrupted impatiently. 'How soon could you set up the appointment?'

His luxuriant black lashes lifted on surprised dark golden eyes. 'As soon as you like?'

'I have to wait more than a week to see my GP, so

it would suit me very well to visit a specialist sooner,' Tabby confided in a rush. 'I'm suffering from terrible nausea and maybe something could be done to alleviate that.'

'I gather being pregnant hasn't been a fun experience so far,' Aristide remarked, still carefully choosing his every word with a caution that irritated her. It struck her that she preferred Aristide relaxed and outspoken because anything else felt fake.

'Not so as you'd notice,' she agreed. 'So, if you organise this obstetrician, we should exchange phone numbers.'

Getting the message that she wanted to return to the bakery, Aristide vaulted upright again and dug out his phone, reminding himself that he had gained more than he had expected from this first visit. She hadn't abused him, assaulted him or refused to speak to him. She was feisty but she could also be reasonable, logical. He would count the meeting a win, a crucial first step on the route he had chosen.

As they reached the street where his bodyguards awaited him, Aristide turned back to her. 'I have one question but it's controversial—'

But Tabby guessed what that question would be, following on from their clash at his apartment that first night. 'Was I prepared to marry Tore for money?' she whispered back to him. '*Yes*, but probably not for the reason you assume.'

Aristide was taken aback by that accurate guess and he still wanted to know more. 'Maybe you'll tell me about it some day,' he teased, amused at the way she was playing him and holding back on giving answers. He could not recall when that had last happened to him with a woman.

CHAPTER FOUR

THE SPECIALIST'S WAITING room was plush and comfortable and Tabby was so disconcerted by the immediate keen attention their arrival received that Aristide had accompanied her into the consultation before she had had the chance to consider leaving him outside. She hadn't objected to his presence during the blood test and, being of a practical bent, saw no reason why he shouldn't learn the extent of her woes.

Mr Chapman was a middle-aged male in a smart suit and he wasted no time in informing them that her blood test had revealed a surprise, without revealing what that surprise was. In short, he was a showman and it was Tabby's job to mention how very sick she had been feeling while he nodded without clarifying anything. She went into the room next door to lie down for the ultrasound with the deflated feeling that she would go back to her sister's apartment knowing no more than she had when she had arrived at the hospital. The consultant joined her and Aristide.

'Do you want me to leave?' Aristide asked, taking her aback with that consideration.

'No, my tummy isn't a sensitive area,' she chuckled and then she closed her eyes while the technician fiddled with the transponder wand, clearly unable to begin without the doctor's prompt.

'And this is why you're feeling sick,' she was informed and she opened her eyes.

'There's two of them!' Aristide exclaimed with all the drama of a male told she was hosting an alien invasion in her stomach.

Tabby suppressed a sigh of concern. Two babies instead of one was an even larger challenge to accept but she was determined not to get anxious. 'I'm a twin…'

'You didn't tell *me* that your sister was a twin,' Aristide complained, but it seemed a moot point as he was asking Mr Chapman questions about what he could see on the screen. She almost contradicted him because she had told him early on when he probably hadn't been listening with much interest.

They emerged from the hospital, both of them sort of shell-shocked in their own different ways.

'In two days, we'll know what we're having,' Aristide proclaimed with unconcealed awe at the blood test that would eventually reveal all facts to them. 'Boys, girls, a mix…'

'New tech is amazing,' Tabby agreed, shaken once again by his attitude, so foreign to her every expectation of him. It occurred to her that it was almost as though Aristide Romanos would welcome the birth of a child in spite of his manwhore reputation. Of course, the one did not automatically exclude the other, her brain warned her. He *could* be a playboy who loved children, couldn't he be?

'You'll have to move into my London apartment,' Aristide told her without stopping to draw breath.

'I beg your pardon?' Tabby queried with a dropped jaw as she clambered into the limo awaiting them.

'Well, obviously, you're not likely to be in a position where you can manage alone,' Aristide countered.

'The consultant didn't say anything like that,' Tabby protested.

'He said you were likely to suffer more severe side effects to being pregnant than other women,' Aristide reminded her. 'Which means that you will need more support to remain healthy and you haven't got any support right now with both your mother and your sister out of the country. Naturally, as the father of the children, it is my responsibility to help—'

'No, I don't see it that way at all,' Tabby argued vehemently as she fastened the seat belt he had helpfully threaded round her as if she couldn't find the belt for herself. 'I don't need anyone's help. I have a job and a home—'

'Your sister's home,' Aristide slotted in grimly.

'Yes, my sister's home *and* a job. I don't need *anyone*—' least of all you, went tactfully unsaid '—to take responsibility for me. I'm completely content managing alone.'

'But you're underweight and sick all the time—'

'Heavens, I shouldn't have let you *be* in the same room with the consultant!' Tabby told him in complete exasperation. 'You sucked all that info in and swallowed it like it was the Holy Grail or something! Let's be realistic here. Some women breeze through pregnancy like it's nothing, others have it less comfy—'

'Yes, but there are valid reasons for you to be less comfy, as you put it...you are carrying *two* babies, not just one. And you are more at risk of complications as well,' Aristide overruled without hesitation.

'But that's nothing to do with you!' Tabby shot back at him furiously. 'Me and my body are not your business!'

'You are going to be the mother of my children,' Aristide contradicted with his perfect measured diction, guaranteed to set her teeth on edge. 'How can that be none of *my* business?'

'Well, it's not!' Tabby assured him in fierce rebuttal. 'We're not a couple, we're not in a relationship—'

'If not a relationship, what is this?' Aristide cut in heatedly to demand.

Tabby pondered. 'A hate fest,' she pronounced with satisfaction. 'We don't even like each other, Aristide. So please do not ever refer to me again as the future mother of your children.'

'I do not hate or dislike you, *angelos mou*.' Aristide breathed in deep and long and resisted the temptation to admit that right now she was irritating the hell out of him. She was being insulting. Of course, she would be the mother of his children. That was going to happen whether she liked it or not and he wasn't going anywhere. Was her outlook tit for tat? He had accused her of unsavoury behaviour that one and only night, *that night* that had been the hottest experience of his life, they had been together. All he had wanted to do since then was repeat the experience, an idea that logic warned him would be as welcome as a rockfall on her in the mood she was in.

'Well, I'm afraid I can't say the same,' Tabby bit out, feeling the backs of her eyes sting with tears, hating the surging hormones that seemed to be making her so uncharacteristically touchy, short-tempered and overly emotional. It was an irony to accept that she could have dealt with Aristide much better without those extra hormones.

Aristide breathed in deep and slow a second time. 'I owe you an apology for the manner in which I behaved that night. We had, I thought, moved past that but I can see that was far too optimistic a belief in these circumstances—'

'Or maybe you just don't like saying sorry,' Tabby cut in before she could bite her tongue and swallow that unnecessarily provocative response. Couldn't she even allow him to apologise?

'You're correct. I don't. But I am sorry about what I said and how I behaved,' Aristide conceded grimly, sounding as if the very words were strangling in his throat.

'Shut up,' she muttered. 'You're just annoying me more—'

'That would seem to be a mutual affliction,' Aristide framed, suddenly closer than ever, leaning over her, evidently having released his seat belt.

He lifted a lean long-fingered brown hand and slowly tucked a hank of pale blonde hair behind her ear, fingertips grazing the top of her delicate ear. And it shouldn't have felt erotic but somehow it *was* erotic, particularly with those smouldering dark golden black-fringed eyes locked to hers. 'Aristide?' she mumbled unevenly, her heart pounding like crazy inside her, liquid heat pushing up between her thighs.

His sensual mouth came down on hers like a silencer that burned her alive with passion. It wasn't like the other kisses he had given her weeks earlier, it was infinitely more hungry, urgent and *fierce*. A flame seemed to spark low in her belly and suddenly, literally, between one moment and the next, she couldn't get enough of him. Her hands clutched at him on a frantic surge of feeling that pushed out everything that had happened before it. There was only that moment, her fingers spearing into his luxuriant black curly hair, a fever beat of insane responses thumping inside her head. *I want you, I hate you, I want you.* And yet the whole time, she was aware of nothing but the sheer burning glory of his mouth on hers, his body weighting hers down, the thrill of that connection setting every nerve ending and skin cell alight.

With an effort, his breathing fractured, Aristide wrenched himself away from her again and flung himself back to his corner of the seat. He didn't have sex with women in the middle of an argument—he didn't *have* arguments with women, didn't get involved enough for that. Yes, he was lost and adrift in this entirely new scenario and it was *brutal*, he decided, awesomely aware of the throbbing pressure behind his zip, the tightness of the constraining fabric. Angry conflict consumed him and plunged him into brooding silence.

Tabby blinked like a sleepwalker roused without warning and only then registered that she was lying full length along the limo passenger seat. How had he achieved that without her noticing? Did it matter? Why was she acting like the sort of woman who said yes and then changed her mind when she *hadn't* changed her mind? For several moments—and she didn't know how many—she had wanted Aristide with every bone and sinew in her body. *Not* her brain. In fact her brain had had nothing whatsoever to do with it, she conceded in dismay.

'That wasn't a good idea,' Aristide murmured tautly.

'You're telling me!' Tabby scoffed in agreement, although his comment had surprised her. What had he truly intended when he had said that she should move into his apartment? A weird platonic relationship and nothing more? It was strange how wounding that suspicion was, she acknowledged. Somewhere in the turmoil of her buzzing thoughts, it seemed, it had proved oddly comforting to be able to believe that Aristide still saw her as desirable even though she was now pregnant and looking less than her best.

Instinct told Aristide to back off but there were other question marks darkening his horizon like storm clouds. He genuinely did not want the mother of his unborn twins to be financially dependent on Tore Renzetti. And yet, that was what would happen if Tabby became reliant on her newly rich sister. But those would be his children, nobody else's, and Aristide could not abide the concept of anyone else taking care of what was most definitely *his*. He needed to lure Tabby fully across to his side of the fence *before* those kids were born. And there was only one stratagem likely to lead to that conclusion. Just as Tabby had once condemned a pregnancy entrapment as an old-fashioned trick, Aristide's solution was an equally dated stratagem.

'I still want you to move into my apartment. It's not even as if I'm always there. I travel a lot. I own properties in other places. If you don't want to live in my apartment, let me buy you a house in your own name to give you and my children basic security,' he breathed in a raw undertone.

Tabby's head was banging with the sheer tension they had both unleashed inside the limousine. She lifted both hands in a desperate silencing motion.

'You're barking up the wrong tree with all of this, Aristide,' she muttered awkwardly. 'Please don't think that I'm not grateful for your willingness to be so generous. But the truth is, I don't need you right now in *any* way! I may be young but I'm not stupid. I'm single and educated and I already have a roof over my head and employment. I appreciated the specialist visit today for the sake of my pregnancy and health. Thank you for organising that for me but anything *more*—'

A hand closed over hers as the limo drew back up outside the bakery. 'Tabby...you're not listening to me—'

Tabby snatched her hand free. 'No, because I don't *need* to listen to you. I don't *need* contact with you either until the twins are born. And, you know, when you start laying down the law in that so bossy style of yours, I'm freakin' grateful I don't have to listen to a word you say!'

'You're being unreasonable,' he snapped back at her.

'And you're being impulsive and not thinking facts through,' Tabby condemned, by now standing on the pavement and looking down into the car to answer him back. 'We're nothing to each other, ships that were meant to pass and then wrecked on each other instead,' she fumbled, conscious they could be overheard now for the first time and lowering her voice.

'But I want *more*,' Aristide bit out with wrathful emphasis.

'Aristide...' Tabby dealt him a pained appraisal. 'You've got women raining all round you—'

An ebony brow hitched. *'Raining?'*

'It's a stupid song reference... OK? But it fits your lifestyle,' she argued. 'Twins *won't* and neither would I, so don't try to suck me into some situation that can only become messy. Do us both a favour. Forget my name, my number and my condition and get on with your own freedom-loving life!'

'Are you trying to say that you won't even accept me *keeping* my own children?' Aristide growled as he swung out of the car, once more in attack-force mode, lean bronzed face taut and clenched hard. He infuriated her by following her to the street door of the upstairs apartment and her teeth grated together. She wanted someone to call him off, deal with him for her before she exploded on him with rage. Unfortunately, Aristide Romanos had probably been born refusing to take polite hints.

He was so stubborn and strong-willed that he made her want to tear her hair out and scream. If he didn't hear what he wanted to hear, he kept on at her. He had no off switch, no concept of personal space or restraint. In every way, Aristide was anathema to her and yet, for some strange reason, she still understood his frustration with her, his inability to realise where she was coming from. She reckoned that he had never met with a brick-wall rejection from a woman before. Without a doubt, he was hugely popular with women. Her online snooping had revealed that as fact. Aristide had it *all*. The looks, the wealth, the charm…when he sought to use it.

'Isn't that my choice?'

'No, it's not. Men have legal rights over their children too—'

'But we're not married!' Tabby objected, surprise at his contention flickering through her.

'We don't have to be in today's world.' Aristide smiled down at her with sudden amusement. 'You didn't know that?'

'How would I know it? I don't have kids or married friends or even friends who have children. There's only my sister, who is adopting,' she conceded uncertainly.

'I will want shared custody rights,' Aristide told her almost conversationally.

Tabby swallowed hard on that enervating warning. All of a sudden he was making parenting with him a challenge she had not expected to have to meet and she was blaming herself for not consulting the law beforehand.

'Pushing me away won't get rid of me,' Aristide warned her.

'Could we talk tomorrow or the next day?' Tabby's courage had petered out the longer he talked because he was so poised, so assured of his rights and legal status, while she knew nothing. 'I have to work both days but my evenings are free.'

'As you like,' Aristide conceded, although he was not in the mood to give way on any point she had raised, but he did see that giving both of them a breathing space could be a good idea. 'Where, the day after tomorrow?'

'Perhaps we could meet at your apartment?' Tabby suggested, keen not to entertain him upstairs again. 'If you give me your address, I'll meet you there at...?'

'Eight,' Aristide decreed.

And that was that. Aristide strode back to his vehicle and she breathed in deep and tried to go on with her working day without dwelling on the shocks that had come her way.

Twins, *two* babies instead of one. Her heartbeat quickened and her insides softened as she remembered the little flashing dots and dark shapes on-screen. And the sheer surprise of learning that Aristide Romanos evidently intended to play the committed father. No, she hadn't expected that, no, she hadn't expected that ambition at all from a male like him. Naturally, that discovery made her less hostile towards him. Nobody knew better than Tabby what a resentful, angry didn't-want-to-be-a-father felt like.

A couple of days later, Violet made a brief visit, Tore and her having suffered a temporary falling-out. Tore Renzetti arrived hotfoot in her wake, clutching a magnificent bouquet, and Tabby left them to mend fences in privacy. Her sister had fallen for the guy and, seemingly, he was all in too. That relieved much of Tabby's guilt on her twin's behalf. The business marriage that Tabby had dreaded had worked out beautifully, it seemed, for Violet.

That evening, clad in the same dress she had worn to their dinner date, Tabby arrived at Aristide's apartment. The garment was loose and comfortable and that was sufficient for her at present when every other decent outfit seemed to be getting too tight round the waist or across the bust. For the first time in her life, she had breasts that were large enough to be noticeable.

Aristide's apartment was much swankier than she had taken the time to appreciate the night she had accompanied him home and that recollection made her face flush red. A manservant greeted her at the door and showed her into a big, open space with a fabulous view of the London skyline and the River Thames.

As she accepted a glass of water and stood admiring the view, Aristide joined her. He wasn't wearing his usual formal business suit. Instead, his lean, muscular physique was sheathed in tight jeans and an open-neck black shirt, a combination that made him look younger and more approachable.

And incredibly sexy, she acknowledged inwardly, taking in the full effect of his lean bronzed features as he smiled at her and her whole body was engulfed in what felt like a hot flush. Perspiration beaded her short upper lip. She glanced hurriedly away from his ripped, powerful physique, sipping her cooling water while promising herself that she would stay in full, unimpeded control of both her body and her swirling emotions. That was the way forward for her and Aristide, she reasoned. They would make sure that they respected each other's boundary lines and, in that way, keep the peace.

'Take a seat,' he urged.

Having spent most of the day on her feet, Tabby sank gratefully down into the nearest armchair. 'Let's try not to fight this time,' she murmured wryly.

'Something tells me that we were born to fight,' Aristide countered. 'We're both determined and we both like our own way better than anyone else's.'

'Maturity has made me more flexible,' Tabby declared.

What maturity? Aristide almost dared to joke as she sat there, slight and small as a child in the seat. 'You seem tired.'

'The delights of early pregnancy,' she quipped ruefully.

'You don't *have* to work—'

'Yes, I do. This is my life, not yours,' Tabby reminded him gently. 'I'm perfectly content for you to take an interest *after* the children are born, but anything more at this stage falls under the heading of interference...and I don't appreciate that approach.'

'I have a suggestion to make,' Aristide informed her.

Tabby tensed, reckoning that a suggestion from Aristide would ultimately prove as serious and immovable as a royal command. She lifted her chin, striving to seem as though she were a receptive audience when she didn't feel as if she could be.

Aristide stalked over to the window, bred-in-the-bone fluid grace edging his every lithe movement. He swung round, brilliant dark golden eyes pinning her in place. 'We need to get to know each other better. We can't be at each other's throats while we are trying to raise children together,' he told her grimly.

'Well, I certainly hope it won't be as bad as that.' Tabby swallowed with difficulty at that challenging opener of a dialogue. 'I think you're talking about a scenario that happens in an ideal world but unfortunately we don't live in that version,' she completed uncomfortably, unable to comprehend getting to know Aristide better in their current non-relationship.

'But if we are *both* willing to make the effort to become accustomed to each other, it *is* achievable.'

While we're trying to raise children together. That single phrase sounded like the bell of doom clanging in Tabby's delicate ears. She wasn't ready to establish *any* kind of togetherness with Aristide. She expected to have to consult him about matters relating to their children and that would be that. His expectations, however, clearly were higher than her own.

'For that reason I suggest that you accompany me to Greece for a couple of weeks, meet my family, learn the lie of the land in my home,' Aristide drawled casually. 'Our children *will* be spending time in Greece.'

Tabby's head flipped round, her blue eyes very wide in sheer shock and surprise. 'My word, I wasn't expecting that invitation! It's a lovely idea *but—*'

'I don't want to hear why you can't do it... I want to hear that you can and will make that effort.'

Tabby winced, her teeth gritting. 'Right now it isn't possible. With the best will in the world, I'm taking care of my sister's business—'

'And I could put a manager in there tomorrow... or *she* could,' Aristide sliced in without hesitation. 'Take that responsibility away and there is no longer anything tying you to the UK for the immediate future.'

'I couldn't let you do that—'

'Why not? You're exhausted. You need a break. Your health and well-being should come first right now,' Aristide told her unarguably.

'I believe that it could be very awkward meeting your family for the first time when I'm pregnant and I'm not even your girlfriend,' Tabby pointed out in a strained and stiff undertone, keen not to offend him.

'Then we should present ourselves as an engaged couple. That's the conventional answer to our predicament. Surely that would make you feel more comfortable and less ill-at-ease?'

Tabby was stunned by the concept. '*Fake* an engagement, you mean?'

'Why not? A fair proportion of engagements don't make it as far as the wedding,' Aristide countered with glancing cynicism. 'I don't see any harm in a pretence of that nature while we're in Greece. We can let the arrangement die away naturally a few months down the road...but in the short term, it would strengthen your position in my life. Family and friends respect ties of that nature.'

In a sudden movement, Tabby stood up tall and studied him with accusing blue eyes. In her own mind's eye, she saw herself transformed from the foolish young woman who had had a one-night fling with Aristide and, unfortunately from his point of view, managed to conceive, to a young woman in control of her life. It was a seductive image even though she knew it wasn't and wouldn't be genuine or real. She compressed her lips, deciding that his intelligence had a positively Machiavellian turn. 'You turn me inside out,' she muttered accusingly. 'You actually have me considering this crazy idea!'

'It's not crazy. You're simply stuck in your little groove and refusing to consider more promising options.'

Tabby ground her teeth together at the reproof but held her tongue. But *was* that how he viewed her? As too conventional and distinctly unadventurous? Her pride was stung. 'All right,' she said curtly. 'If we can get the bakery covered in time and Violet is happy with that decision, I'll go to Greece with you.'

Aristide's dark eyes glittered like gold ingots in strong sunlight, satisfaction winging through him in an intoxicating wave. He knew that he was being manipulative and he really didn't feel an atom of regret. Within days, he'd have a ring on her finger. A man could not afford to baulk at a solid wall of resistance, he had to get across it any way he could.

A sapphire, he had decided, a gorgeous sapphire to match those stubborn, sparkling blue eyes. 'Phone your sister and tell her what you want to do and seek her approval,' he advised smoothly. 'I'll concentrate on drumming up replacement managers.'

Refreshments were served. Tea, for her, coffee for him and tiny delectable sandwiches followed by a selection of pastries. Tabby ate with appetite. Her anti-nausea medication was keeping her sickness at bay while encouraging her to eat a little more. She phoned her twin and brought her up to speed while she paced in Aristide's airy hall.

'Greece?' Violet squealed in astonishment. 'Gosh, this is so exciting—'

'No, it's not,' Tabby contradicted. 'It's a pretend engagement, *not* a real one, which is why I decided not to tell Mum about it.'

'I'm not sure I see the point,' her sister disappointed her by admitting. 'I mean, it's not like an engagement ties either of you down legally in any way—'

'It will make me feel better…as if I have some actual status in his life when I meet his family,' Tabby whispered, but only after checking that the door back into Aristide's presence was fully closed. 'But it's all smoke and mirrors this way, isn't it? He knew exactly how to get me fully onboard.'

'I thought you hated him—'

'Well, I do…sometimes,' she adjusted in growing embarrassment.

'Just not *all* the time?' her twin prompted with audible amusement.

'He's right on one score. Neither of us need any added stress or drama right now.'

'Twins!' Violet squealed in sheer anticipation.

'One of whom is definitely a boy,' Tabby reminded her sister, 'but I still have to tell Aristide that I got the call about the blood test today.'

A boy and a girl, one of each, she rather hoped, thinking that that mix would be company for each other as she and Violet had been while each pursuing their own interests.

'A boy,' Aristide repeated minutes later, when she told him the results of the blood test. 'So, I will have possibly two sons or a son and a daughter. When will we know for certain?'

'In another few weeks. I'll need another ultrasound,' she explained, her attention locked to his lean, strong features and the interest unhidden there in the vibrant gleam of his expressive eyes. 'Be warned that you *can* get an erroneous result. The process isn't foolproof.'

Nobody knew that better than Aristide but DNA was unarguable fact. And *this* time, he knew, he knew for certain that he could not entertain for even a second the suspicion that those two babies would not be of his blood. He didn't care what sex the twins were, only that they were Romanos children. 'My relatives will be shaken by this development and I will warn them in advance of our arrival.'

'Shaken?' Tabby queried that choice of word, smothering a yawn at the exhaustion already creeping up on her again. These nights she always ended up in bed much earlier than had once been her habit.

'A long time ago, I swore that I would stay single and have no children,' Aristide admitted after a pause for thought, finally deeming it acceptable to tell her that much, even if he had no plans to tell her the rest of that sordid little story.

Her smooth brow furrowed. 'Why on earth would you make such a far-reaching statement at what must've been such a young age?'

Aristide shrugged a broad shoulder. 'Maybe I'll tell you some day. I'm not someone who looks back with regret. I prefer to look forward and I *was* still a student when I first reached that decision. Now let me see you safely home.'

And he did and she crawled into bed. She thought about his admission that he had once decided to remain unmarried and childless. She frowned, wondering at the past unhappy relationship that must surely have dredged such a declaration from a young man. He had got hurt once, badly hurt, she suspected with a pang of belated sympathy.

For the first time Tabby was feeling a little less alone. Her mother was excited and simultaneously worried about her elder daughter's pregnancy. Naturally the older woman was more preoccupied with her treatment plan. In addition, phone conversations were no replacement for talking face to face, Tabby conceded. Violet's main focus in life was Tore and Belle, her own little family.

But Aristide was different. He was focused solely on her. He was trying, she could see that, and he deserved that she made an equal effort. So, she resolved, no more sniping, no more eyeing him up like a steak dinner, either. But she still slid into sleep fondly remembering Aristide's smile at the prospect of a son and daughter or any combination of children and marvelled at his enthusiasm. She was lucky, she told herself. Unlike her own father, Aristide truly *wanted* children. In comparison, Sam Blessington had felt trapped and diminished by fatherhood and domesticity.

The following few days were exceptionally busy. Interviews, which Violet joined, took place and a female replacement was chosen and deemed suitable to start working immediately by Tabby's side.

At the start of the next week, Aristide sent his car to waft her to his apartment again to look at the engagement ring. Tabby couldn't understand why she should even see it in advance as a ring would only be an accessory that she would naturally return to him when the fake engagement concluded. Aristide pointed out that she was the party who would have to wear it and her text protests died down.

You argue about every little thing

Thinking that he was getting his own way enough that she could expect him to understand her reservations, Tabby arrived at his apartment, flushed and annoyed. Straight away she was ushered into the lounge where a jeweller and a security guard were hovering in readiness. A small box was set and clicked open for her perusal. It contained a dazzling blue ring in an unusual setting, an oval in a stunning diamond surround. It was breathtaking.

'Try it on for size,' the jeweller remarked with enthusiasm as he removed it from the box, gave it an unnecessary polish and extended it to her. 'A sapphire from Kashmir, rare and much appreciated by all who know their gems.'

Aristide watched the ring he had selected for her glide onto her slender finger in a perfect fit. 'It's the same cornflower blue as your eyes,' he told her.

'It's different and very elegant,' Tabby said, a little breathless as the sunlight accentuated the colourful depth of the precious gem and it shone, holding out her hand, daring to smile for the first time at him.

A slashing smile of appreciation illuminated his lean dark face, emphasising his stunningly handsome features. The level brows, high cheekbones, cut jaw line and brilliant charismatic dark golden eyes. And for a split second, time froze for Tabby while she stared back at him, involuntarily fascinated by all that set Aristide apart from other men.

'The stylist is waiting for you in my guest room,' he informed her in an aside.

Conscious of their audience, Tabby assumed that he wanted to deal with the business of buying the ring with her elsewhere and she said nothing about the sudden reference to a stylist, who presumably styled, whatever that entailed.

Bare minutes later, Tabby was surrounded by rails of clothes and the extrovert stylist was dragging out and holding clothes up for her scrutiny while her assistant proffered accessories and other combinations of garments, both women chattering volubly at the same time. All the garments were acceptable in cut to act as early maternity wear, she was assured.

'You can't buy me clothes,' she declared acidly to Aristide in the aftermath. 'I was ambushed.'

'That was the plan. Like the ring, they're mere props,' Aristide proclaimed dismissively. 'To act like my fiancée, you have to look as though you belong in my life…and unless you're happy to play Cinderella for your audience, you can't do that in unadorned cotton.'

CHAPTER FIVE

Ushered onto the private jet, Tabby attempted not to gape at the gorgeous pale pearl leather upholstery or the number of hovering staff who had greeted her as she climbed the steps to board.

She looked the part of a passenger on such a luxury flight, she reckoned with relief, well aware that her smart green dress and light jacket, which were cut to flatter the increase in her bust and waist measurements, would look stylish in any company. Even walking through the airport, she had registered that a mere flash of her dazzlingly noticeable engagement ring was sufficient to make her conspicuous to many people.

'You look terrific,' Aristide drawled with quiet approval, revelling in her newly found poise. 'I also feel a little less likely to be accused of cradle-snatching!'

'I'm almost twenty-two!' Tabby objected.

'And I'm almost twenty-nine. It's enough of a gap to cause comment,' Aristide told her, veiled eyes roaming slowly over her as she sank into the seat opposite him, slender, shapely legs set at a graceful angle to one side.

'Did your family comment?'

'Only to tease me about younger women,' he acknowledged with amusement.

'I think it's time you tell me who makes up your family,' she responded nervously. 'I only have Mum, Violet and Belle in my corner and you already know all about them. My grandfather doesn't really count because Violet and I've never got to know him...and what we do know isn't good.'

'My only really close relative is my father, but he has several brothers and sisters, who have given me a squad of cousins. My father's on his fifth marriage and my stepmother, Andy, has stood the test of time, unlike her predecessors. They've been married ten years now.'

'Andy?' she questioned.

'It's short for Andromeda. She's a darling, who would've made a great substitute mother for me, had she been around when I was younger and still needed one,' Aristide confided. 'I'm fond of her.'

'What happened to your own mother?' she asked uncertainly.

'She was my father's first wife,' Aristide informed her ruefully. 'She died from a fall on the stairs when I was only a few months old.'

'I'm so sorry,' Tabby muttered with a wince, blue eyes awash with sympathy. 'Do you have any memory of her?'

'None whatsoever,' Aristide admitted with regret. 'My earliest memories only relate to nannies, stepmothers or my father's temporary lovers.'

Her brow furrowed. 'Temporary?'

'The lovers, even the other wives, were all of a temporary ilk until my father met Andy. Dad's liaisons lasted weeks or a couple of months but, sometimes, only days,' Aristide related with a pained look of recollection stamping his lean dark face. 'My father is or *was* a dysfunctional man when it came to the women in his life. But he's settled now and content in his marriage.'

Tabby nodded. 'That's good. What about siblings?'

'None. I'm still an only child but I do have a few stepsisters and stepbrothers, whom I still view as family members. Some of their mothers were rather unreliable and my father maintained close ties with them, no matter how bitter the break-ups were.'

'What's your relationship like with your father?' Tabby was enjoying herself, delighting in Aristide's new openness with her and his willingness to satisfy her curiosity.

'At times, it's been troubled,' Aristide admitted, his shapely mouth compressing as he spoke with yet more honesty than she had expected to receive from him. 'For a long time I blamed Demetrius for the unstable home I grew up in with all those different women coming and going. I was a very pious teenager.' He grimaced at the memory. 'At one point, we didn't speak for several years. But adulthood made me less judgemental. He did fall for some truly horrendous women, however. He also cheated on some decent ones. Maybe he just wasn't ready to fully commit again until he met Andy.'

'And how does he feel about this pretend engagement of ours?' she steeled herself to ask.

'Nobody but us *knows* that it's fake,' he reminded her in stark reproof. 'He's shocked and surprised but very excited about the prospect of two grandkids. The stepchildren are all younger than I am. You will be the first in the family to reproduce. Now tell me about *your* father.'

'He's a creep,' Tabby admitted without hesitation. 'He never wanted children and if he'd had a choice, it wouldn't have been what he referred to as "whiny" daughters. I haven't seen him since the divorce and that's six, no, seven years ago. He tied Mum up in court for months because he fiercely resented being expected to support us and he didn't want further contact with either of us. We're just grateful that he's out of our lives now.'

'You're making me appreciate that I could have had it a lot worse. Demetrius has always loved and defended me. Whatever else he was, he has always been a great father. Clearly, I was fortunate, *angelos mou*.'

'Better the devil you know,' Tabby teased, watching that smile like summer sunlight flash across his lips, elevating his cheekbones and lightening his eyes to scorching gold enticement. She saw the approaching stewardess perform a double take at his sheer masculine appeal in that moment. Colouring on her own behalf for her hyper-awareness of Aristide, she listened as a wide variation of refreshments was offered.

As she collided involuntarily with his eyes, a little shimmy of heat currented down from her belly, making her squeeze her thighs together, much as if she was afraid of that sexual response somehow escaping her. It was little wonder that she was so susceptible, she reasoned. Aristide was drop-dead gorgeous, particularly with his lean muscular physique shown to advantage in beige tailored chinos and a dark purple shirt open at his strong brown throat. Naturally she was still attracted to him. Nothing that physically intense magically evaporated like mist.

'So, where in Greece are we heading?'

'Anthos, the island where my mother and I were both born. Her family has always been based there,' he explained. 'My father has made Anthos his home too.'

Somewhere in the aftermath of a light lunch, Tabby shifted as Aristide lifted her into his arms to carry her on board a helicopter, where he fixed headphones to her head and fastened her seat belt for her before sitting down.

'Where are we?' she mumbled, barely opening her heavy eyes.

'Almost at our destination,' he promised.

The jolt of the helicopter landing again woke her

and she surfaced in a tizzy, peering out of a window to note the sprawling white house on the hillside below the hot blue sky. It was massive, an undeniable mansion in size, and people were already gathering on the spacious front veranda. In dismay she sat up and dug into her bag to search frantically for a comb and a lipstick. A cool, restraining hand covered hers. 'You look great,' Aristide told her soothingly, and he was telling her the truth because she might look rumpled and a little sleepy but she was still indisputably beautiful. 'There's no need for you to primp when we've been travelling for hours.'

'This is my property,' Aristide told her quietly as he vaulted out onto the grass and reached back to lift her down by his side in the sunlight. 'Demetrius and Andy host family parties here because I have more space. Their own home, my former childhood home, is on the other side of the island, so there is no need for you to feel like a guest here.'

As they walked down a grassy path, Tabby noticed many of the guests standing outside disperse back indoors at a small, bustling brunette's instigation. Aristide, she realised, was the very image of his father and how he might look twenty or thirty years down the road. Demetrius was tall, straight, his black hair winged with grey, undeniably handsome and fit, the very image of a silver fox. By his side, his wife, Andy, was a curvy, scarlet-clad brunette with lively dark eyes and an irrepressible smile of welcome.

'Oh, it is *the* ring!' Andy exclaimed in excitement as she caught Tabby's wrist lightly in hers to grab a closer look at the sapphire. 'It's absolutely tremendous, gorgeous!'

'Thanks. I love it,' Tabby admitted with a smile.

'I'll show you up to our room. You can lie down if you like,' Aristide interposed.

'Again?' Tabby stressed with amusement, thinking that he needed to spend a little longer with his father and stepmother. 'I slept most of the way here. I can surely stay awake long enough to meet some people.'

'If that's what you would prefer—'

'Maybe you're gasping to look after an invalid,' she teased with a roll of her eyes. ''Fraid that's not me. All you've got here is one pregnant lady, who's feeling chirpy after so much rest. My nausea is definitely subsiding now. If you were to offer me food—'

'I can help there.' Andy cupped an arm to Tabby's elbow and walked her off into a grand room where a splendid buffet table and a collection of people awaited them. 'I slept the clock around when I was pregnant and I ate regular snacks to stave off the sickness,' she told her. 'Do you realise that Aristide has never brought a woman here with him before?'

'I didn't know that,' Tabby said non-committally, all too well aware that she was visiting because at some stage their twins would be visiting with their father and it was her job to pave the way for that future.

As she was filling a plate, various casual introductions were made. A welter of middle-aged uncles, aunts and more youthful cousins followed. A skinny teenaged girl with bright red hair darted past them to throw her arms round Aristide as he appeared in the doorway.

'Melody, one of my husband's former stepkids,' Tabby's companion explained. 'She and her two brothers lived with Aristide for weeks after their mother left them alone in London, where they attend school. They knew him when they were very young and contacted him when they ran out of money. I think they'll be spending most of the summer with us.'

'I'm glad he stepped in,' Tabby remarked, watching two tall teenage boys join their sister's animated conversation.

'He's good with children,' the brunette said cheerfully. 'Particularly teenagers. We're getting a little too old to be seen as cool.'

'Aristide can be surprising,' Tabby admitted with a sudden smile, suddenly grateful that she had come to Greece to meet his family even if she was a fake fiancée. It was reassuring to be somewhere Aristide could relax and shed his remote and detached business persona.

Making some more food choices with Andy's encouragement, she was soon sitting down and socialising.

'So, tell me about her,' Demetrius Romanos invited his son.

'Not right now. I know how you work. The more I tell you about her, the more suspicious of her you will become,' Aristide countered, knowing his parent of old and too respectful of him to comment that he considered his father one of the last people he would listen to advice from when it came to a woman.

'She *is* a real beauty,' his father conceded. 'But so was the last one—'

'Don't bring Imogen into it,' Aristide sliced in grimly. 'That's old history.'

'She's on the island right now,' his father warned him impatiently. 'I was furious when I was told but her grandfather is dying and she's entitled to visit. However, you own their properties—'

'I've no intention of being that petty,' Aristide parried, his lean, strong face taut. 'Let sleeping dogs lie.'

'As long as the dog doesn't start barking and upset her replacement—'

'Tabby's *not* a replacement. Tabby's an entirely different kind of woman,' Aristide murmured with innate assurance. 'If you take the time to talk to her, you will realise that.'

In between conversations, Tabby sipped her tea and watched Aristide with his father, wondering what they were discussing because she could see Aristide's hackles rising and his parent's unapologetic stance.

'They argue…frequently,' Andromeda Romanos whispered in rueful warning. 'But I've only once seen it come to an exchange of blows—'

'Oh, my goodness...' Tabby's eyes rounded in dread.

'I shouldn't have mentioned it,' the older woman said equally quickly. 'It only happened that once and tempers had become very frayed, I'm afraid. That incident separated them for years, so it won't *ever* happen again. They're far too fond of each other to risk it.'

'I'm relieved to hear that because I grew up in a violent home. My father drank and he often took his temper out on us,' she confided.

'How on earth did you and your mother cope?'

'Well, ultimately we didn't. They divorced years ago.'

Shortly after that exchange, Aristide retrieved her and offered to show her round the house. Some visitors were leaving, a few were staying over until the following day and some, like the former stepchildren, were staying at his father's house.

'It's a huge house,' Tabby commented as they stood in the giant hall with its contemporary limestone floor and modern paintings. 'Did you inherit it?'

'No. I built it during the period my father and I were at odds,' Aristide confided with a wince. 'I was only twenty and I was showing off—'

Tabby grinned as he directed her towards the glass and stone double-flight staircase. 'You? Showing off? I don't believe it!' she mocked.

'It's far too big and unless I have half a dozen

kids, I'll never fill it. It doesn't have much character either—'

'So why did you build it?'

'It was petty,' Aristide said wryly. 'But I was reminding my father that I was totally independent. I inherited my mother's wealth and this island on the day she died. I've never had to fight or ask or struggle for anything, which is why I went into business. I needed the challenges.'

Tabby sighed. 'My life has been so different from yours. Growing up, we were always struggling for money. Mum wasn't well enough educated to get a decent job and what she did earn my father tended to take off her. He was always moaning about how his family sucked his artistic soul out of him,' she muttered with a curled lip. 'But I don't believe he had an artistic soul. That was his excuse for ignoring the bills for rent, electricity and food and all the rest of the stuff you need to cover to survive.'

'No wonder you were willing to marry a stranger for cash!' Aristide said, startling her rigid with that assumption.

'Oh, good heavens, no, is that what you think? But that wasn't why I was willing to marry Tore Renzetti. No, *that* was to pay for Mum's clinical trial in Massachusetts and cover her costs while she was there. It's taken every penny of it too because Violet and I wanted to know she would be comfortable,' she explained. 'And she hasn't known what it is to be comfortable very often since she left my grandfather's home to marry my father.'

In receipt of her explanation, Aristide froze into stillness on the landing, his lean, powerful frame suddenly rigid with tension as he vented a harsh exclamation in Greek. 'Why the hell didn't you tell me about your *mother's* need to pay for her treatment weeks ago?' he demanded in raw disbelief.

'It wasn't relevant to us...and anyway, Violet ended up having to marry Tore instead, so it wasn't really my story to tell any more,' she proffered uncomfortably. 'And I hope that I can trust you to keep those facts quiet. Now that my sister and Tore have fallen for each other and are staying together, I shouldn't think either of them would want that original story told.'

'I'm not going to discuss it with anyone,' Aristide declared curtly. 'I'm just furious that you threw Renzetti's existence in my face that night and you all but encouraged me to think the very worst of you!'

Tabby shrugged a slight shoulder, not quite sure why he was so annoyed with her. 'Well, I had to throw back something with all the accusations you were hurling,' she reasoned defensively. 'And I believed that telling you I was to marry Tore and that *he* was wealthy would relieve you of the fear that you'd been specially targeted by me for some sort of profit venture—'

'But it also made me believe that you were a

cheat!' Aristide flung back at her in condemnation. 'And I don't like people who cheat on their partners!'

Surprised by his vehemence and the fierce burnished gold of his gaze, Tabby flinched and spread her hands slowly in a soothing gesture. 'I've never cheated on anyone. I'm sorry if I misled you but it was accidental—'

'If you hadn't misled me, I'd have been in touch with you far sooner than I was,' Aristide shot at her, faint colour now edging his hard cheekbones while emotion still flared like a storm warning in his dark golden eyes, his annoyance and embarrassment visible. 'Sometimes, you really can be a piece of work!'

'I've apologised,' Tabby reminded him flatly. 'Have the grace to accept it and move on…'

Aristide closed a hand over hers and stalked down the long landing to the double doors at the foot, throwing a door wide. 'This is the master suite for our use.'

'Our?' Tabby questioned, kicking off her shoes that were pinching a little and stepping back to take in the full impressive span of the spacious bedroom and the selection of doors that opened off it. It was a really lovely room done in masculine shades of silver grey and dark blue, but the giant bed festooned in silvery drapes and crisp white linen would have delighted any princess in search of a suitable setting.

'Well, obviously we're sharing,' Aristide pointed out.

Tabby had assumed they would be sharing a bedroom and had refused to think about what that would be like. But now Aristide had started criticising her behaviour and had riled her up into a mood. *'Obviously?'* she stressed out of badness and as Aristide's eyes flamed like torches, she lifted a brow. 'There's a very nice couch over there. You could use that.'

'Like hell I will!' Aristide fired back at her.

Tabby gave him a tight little smile and rested her hands down on her hips for emphasis. 'Right at this minute, you have made me so mad with you that you're condemned to the couch—'

'I'm not sleeping anywhere but in that bed *with* you!' Aristide framed.

'Andy mentioned dinner and that I could change into something more relaxed,' Tabby announced, ignoring that statement as she shifted the subject. *'After you unzip my dress…'*

The grudging hint of an appreciative smile tugged at the corners of Aristide's sensual mouth. 'Turn around,' he instructed.

Tipping off her jacket, Tabby acquiesced. The zip ran down, the edges parted, cooler air brushing her heated skin. Lips pressed in a brief, light salute to her slender spine and she gasped, an electrified shiver running through her entire body. He set her back from him and murmured in a husky undertone, 'Don't pretend that you're not feeling the same things I'm feeling, *angelos mou*.'

In instant denial of the charge, Tabby spun round. 'The couch is still yours,' she countered.

'I need a shower,' Aristide breathed in a driven undertone. 'This room has separate bathrooms and dressing rooms, enabling both of us to have our privacy.'

And she needed a shower too, Tabby reflected dizzily, reliving the chemical charge of his carnal mouth on her warm skin, another reflexive shiver rippling through her taut and aroused body. Because there it was, that ferocious attraction that she would have denied but that honesty made her admit... She wanted to rip his clothes off, pin him to that bed and have her thoroughly wicked way with him. But surely that phase of their relationship was over and done with, wasn't it? Why was it that she had waited for so long to have a sexual relationship and the minute she tasted the flavour of sex with Aristide, she wanted more, more, *more*? It mortified her to feel like that around him.

In the bathroom he showed her, she found her toiletries already arranged and she smiled in surprise, realising that while she had been downstairs someone had unpacked her luggage for her. She stripped and walked into the shower to freshen up, drying herself on a fresh fleecy towel and reflecting that the life of a jet-setter certainly offered its comforts. With a touch of gloss on her lips and mascara, she was done. Carefully wrapped in the towel, she ventured into the spacious custom-built dressing room next door where her clothing selection for her two weeks in sunny Greece looked ridiculously tiny. She picked a casual long skirt and a tee that skimmed forgivingly over her no longer flat midriff.

Aristide, clad in well-fitted jeans and a tee, surveyed her as she emerged. 'Classy and simple. That's your style and it suits you,' he murmured, disconcerting her. 'And you really don't appreciate the damage you did to my opinion of you when you allowed me to believe that you were a money-grabbing cheat.'

'I didn't care that night,' Tabby countered, lifting her chin. 'As far as I was concerned, I was defending myself the only way I could and back then I still believed that it would be me who had to marry Tore. It wasn't until I realised that I was pregnant, which broke the contract I'd signed, that I thought it would have to be Violet who married him instead.'

'You should always care about what you reveal about yourself,' Aristide censured. 'Even if you're simply trying to score points and particularly if it paints you in bad colours.'

'I didn't give two hoots about your opinion that night, not after what you had said to me!' Tabby flipped back without apology, her head high. 'I have my pride too, Aristide. Why would you suddenly start imagining that I was the kind of woman who would set you up for some sort of a pregnancy trap? Who would want you for your wealth rather than who you are as a person?'

Aristide looked grim, his lean, strong face etched in hard lines. '*Why?* Because something rather similar happened to me once before and that harrowing experience probably left me oversensitive, which is why I lost my temper and assumed the very worst of you.'

Tabby was stunned into silence by that bleak, blunt confession. As she hovered, an apology brimming on her lips, Aristide took charge and urged her to the door. Something similar? *Harrowing* experience? His choice of that particular word shocked her and sobered her into deeper thought. 'Was there a child born?' she heard herself ask under her breath as they headed towards the stairs.

'No, the woman concerned miscarried,' he revealed flatly. 'Now can we talk about something else? I don't want to talk about *that*.'

Typical Aristide, she thought ungraciously. Having finally told her the truth about why he had flown off the handle that first night with her, he was still refusing to share the whole story. But then why should he? His intimate past wasn't her business. He wasn't bound to tell her about everything. Intellectually, she understood and accepted that, but she craved further knowledge of that particular episode because it had clearly left a wound.

Dinner was full of chatter and easy conversation. Demetrius asked her how she had met Aristide and she told him about that day at Traxis and the belated discovery that Aristide was not a senior accountant. He laughed but gave her a searching look, as if he was not quite sure whether or not to believe her.

As the meal continued, Aristide seemed to become more preoccupied and then, over coffee, he rose and gave her an apologetic appraisal. 'I have a visit to make to an old friend this evening. I hope you'll forgive me for leaving you for an hour or so on your first night.'

In an even more sudden movement, Demetrius Romanos stood up as well. 'Old Theo? Of course. I'll come too and pay my respects,' he announced.

And with that, the two men left the room.

'Who's old Theo?' Tabby asked Andromeda curiously.

'A fisherman Aristide knew as a boy. He's dying,' the brunette explained. 'Aristide didn't know that Theo had fallen ill until he arrived.'

Tabby nodded, surprised by the fleeting look of discomfiture on Andromeda's face, wondering if it was dealing with the old man's passing that made her that way or whether there was some other complication that she remained ignorant of.

Aristide returned in a volatile mood. Theo had been well enough to reminisce for almost an hour but then Imogen had joined them and his father had stood up to immediately leave, determined to protect his son to the last even if his son no longer needed protecting. He wasn't a teenager any more, more in love with a woman's face and body than anything else. He no longer expected perfection either, knowing there was no such thing. Everyone had strengths and weaknesses. Imogen had once been his weakness but that was over and done. In her favour, his former fiancée had been irreproachably polite and charming and had not once alluded to the past. Points to her on that score, he acknowledged, knowing his own reactions had been less presentable and his father's comments on her afterwards had been unrepeatable.

In the darkness, as he stripped and left his clothes in an untidy heap, he studied Tabby in the moonlight filtering through the room. Light shimmered over the point of a delicate ear and pale blonde hair as she shifted and rolled over, evidently in the grip of a disturbing dream. A low moan was wrenched from her. 'Daddy...*no!*' she sobbed and his blood chilled in his veins.

She sounded like a frightened child and Aristide was in that bed and gathering her into his arms before he could even think about what he was doing. His need to comfort her was overwhelming.

CHAPTER SIX

TABBY SURFACED SHUDDERING and gasping for breath, her last recollection of trying to intervene after her father had struck her mother to the floor and, while he was still ranting, returned to kick her.

'It's only a dream,' Aristide murmured softly.

'No, it was a memory of Dad beating up Mum and me trying to stop him,' she muttered shakily.

'And how did that go?' Aristide prompted in a strained undertone.

'I got kicked too,' she mumbled wretchedly. 'But he backed off after that.'

'What age were you?'

'Seven, eight… I'm not sure,' she admitted. 'I've never told anyone about that before. I was in bed and I heard him shouting and I got up. I should've known better—'

Aristide expelled his breath in an audible hiss. 'No, he's the one who should have known better when he saw his child in his way. But then he should not have been hurting either you or your mother.'

Aristide cradled her in his big, strong arms as he sat on the bed and she had never felt safer in her life. Dimly she recognised that was always, *always* what she had sought from a male: that he would be there for her when she needed him, that he would understand that she was softer inside than her prickly exterior implied. And then, most of all, that he would make those connections without thinking she was somehow *less*. The scent of Aristide, forest-fresh air with a hint of sea salt, engulfed her and she breathed in deep, firmly resisting the urge to snuggle, aware of the hard male contours of his lean, fit body against her.

'What are you wearing?' she whispered.

'Nothing. I was getting undressed and then you were crying out and I wanted to wake you out of that dream,' he murmured lazily. 'And what are you wearing? Something silky and small.'

Long fingers tugged at the hem of her shorts and she shrank inside her light vest top, her nipples tightening and pushing forward at the awareness that he was naked.

'Rather cruel and tempting considering I'm the guy you were set on sentencing to the couch,' Aristide opined huskily.

'You weren't here. I wasn't thinking of what I was wearing,' she protested truthfully. 'Anyway, I wasn't really planning to make you sleep on the couch. I was just annoyed with you.'

'You smell delicious, *angelos mou*,' Aristide breathed thickly. 'I think I'd better return you to bed.'

Rising, he threw back the sheet and slotted her into place, throwing the sheet over her. Without that physical contact, she felt cold and then he climbed in beside her and she relaxed again as he drew her into his warmth. In a sudden movement, she squirmed round and put her arms round him, her mouth instinctively seeking and finding his. And just as suddenly, she was pinned beneath him and he was kissing her breathless, heat darting to the heart of her and stirring a tight, intolerable ache.

Aristide released her swollen mouth and lifted his dark, curly head. 'You're impulsive,' he pointed out, as if she weren't already conscious of that failing. 'I was sentenced to the couch…remember?'

'I'm not impulsive—'

'You so *are*. I have to know that you want me and that this isn't some impulse you'll start regretting at dawn,' he decreed.

'I always want you,' Tabby admitted as if that was so obvious that it should go without saying.

'And I never stopped wanting you,' Aristide growled.

'Has there been anyone else or several someone elses for you since that night?' she asked, even though she knew that she wasn't being fair demanding an answer to that question when they had parted as enemies without any kind of future even seeming possible.

'There's been nobody since you,' Aristide admitted after a lengthy pause, brilliant eyes glimmering dark in the moonlight. 'But that isn't a fair question—'

'I *know*,' she agreed without regret. 'But I had to know. I'm possessive. I don't share—'

'Neither do I,' Aristide growled, returning to worry at her parted lips with his lips, the edge of his teeth and then the deep plunge of his tongue, his hunger unhidden and thoroughly stimulating.

'Did I ever tell you how much I like the way you kiss?' she asked breathlessly.

'No. You can tell me tomorrow over a late breakfast. I think we are both due a very late breakfast,' Aristide positively purred, the vibration of his deep dark drawl travelling down her taut spine, filtering intrinsically into softer, warmer places.

He settled her on the bed and leant over her, all hard profile and dominance in the low light. 'Have you any idea how sexy it is that you're carrying my children?'

As a big hand splayed possessively across her abdomen, Tabby blinked and shook her head. 'Sexy?' she queried in disbelief because, to date, pregnancy had not felt sexy to her. It had meant tiredness and nausea and the irritatingly strong rise of hormones that craved Aristide and his lean, hard body round the clock, something that torture would not have persuaded her to admit.

'It makes me feel proud, possessive, territorial,

angelos mou,' Aristide husked. 'When I entered that bakery and saw another man fondling your hand—'

'What other man?' she exclaimed.

'The guy in the chef outfit—'

'Oh, you mean Luca, Violet's replacement baker. He's harmless,' she assured him without concern. 'He flirts with every female around him and he's ridiculously touchy-feely.'

'You need to crush that tendency in him. He'll land you with a sexual harassment issue,' Aristide forecast.

Tabby loosed a startled laugh and reached up a hand to cup his hard cheekbone. 'Aristide, all the female staff, no matter what their age, adore Luca because he makes them feel good, he makes them feel interesting. He's a genuinely nice person and you don't meet as many of those as you would like to.'

'But you won't be there any more for him to flirt with,' Aristide affixed, clearly happy at that development. 'You're out of bounds now.'

'Oh, really?'

For the next two weeks, she was thinking.

'I'm the only guy allowed to flirt with you,' Aristide told her.

'Oh, I don't think that's going to work,' she warned with helpless amusement. 'Sometimes a little flirting is what makes the day go around a little faster.'

'Not for you,' Aristide asserted, nuzzling his jaw against the soft silk screening her aching breasts.

She could feel her nipples, tight as buds, straining for attention.

The warmth of his mouth enclosed a pulsing bud below the thin silk and she shuddered, sudden excitement claiming her at even that slight touch.

'And what do I get in return for not flirting?' she dared to gasp as he lifted his head again.

'Me and bragging rights,' Aristide quipped with a lazy, wildly engaging grin. 'Only you can pin me down.'

'That's you assuming that I *want* to pin you down,' Tabby murmured. 'But just like you, that first night I was only after one stolen experience, only we both got more than we bargained for out of it.'

'Why did you only want that?' he demanded.

'Think about it. I didn't want this contracted stranger of a husband to become my first lover,' she argued ruefully. 'It was a stupid, short-sighted move and I soon regretted it—'

'I don't,' Aristide imparted, lifting the vest top off over her head, quickly sliding his attention to her slender hips and skimming down the fabric there as well. 'I met you and I have not a single regret.'

'Seriously?' Tabby gazed up at him in wonder at that statement. 'But you *must* have regrets. You didn't want children—'

'It would be more accurate to say that hurt pride made me deny any desire for children of my own,' Aristide contradicted, lowering his dark tousled head to find the pert buds of her full breasts.

Just as quickly, the concept of talking vanished from Tabby's mind as the erotic invitation of his teasing mouth caught and played with her swollen pink nipples and his lean fingers joined in the torture. Her body writhed under him of its own volition. She was like a touch paper set alight, need burning through her like an arrow, sharp and unsatisfied. She had wanted him for what felt like for ever and now suddenly he was there and nothing could happen fast enough to answer that fierce craving for sensation.

Aristide was intuitive. It was as though he were inside her head, knowing the extent of her desire, working though that to a painfully slow degree down her body to find all the most sensitive spots. She couldn't stay still, racked by hunger and intense urgency. He parted her slender quivering thighs, traced the heart of her with teasing fingertips when she was already too far beyond that stage. As his touch glanced across her swollen clit, she went off like a rocket into an orgasm that shot through her like white lightning, momentarily stilling her before her body jerked and convulsed in pleasure.

Unperturbed, Aristide continued to dally there, utilising his mouth and his tongue and his long fingers with a finesse that sent her shooting a second time into orbit, a deep flush drenching her cheeks as she thought of how easily she had responded and the depth of the need that she had exposed. He had been quite correct when he had accused her of being impulsive, she acknowledged unhappily. She had not even thought about what would happen if she ended up having sex with Aristide again. But did that matter any more? They didn't need a label, she told herself. They were both single and committed only to their unborn children. Perhaps friendship would've been a wiser option but there was little chance of a platonic relationship developing while they were still so wildly attracted to each other.

He held her against him while she still trembled and gasped and struggled for breath. A lean hand ran down the damp curve of her hip and her heartbeat started to edge up in pace again. 'Do you want a break or may I continue?'

A little sensual tingle at her molten core answered and she shifted back into his long, strong body, drinking in the fresh scent of him with pleasure. 'You need to ask?'

Aristide laughed with rich appreciation, claiming her mouth again, tasting her with hungry concision. He ached for her and he crushed her parted lips beneath his, teasing her tender flesh with skilled fingers, probing her slick depths with a satisfied growl. Excitement gripped her again. He could make her want him again so easily that for a split second she felt intimidated. Reacting to that feeling, she slid a hand down over his muscular stomach and found him, velvet over steel, more than ready for her, and he groaned and nipped at the taut muscle between her neck and her shoulder in retribution.

He rearranged her like a doll but there was nothing doll-like about the zing of pure energy surging through her veins or the race of her quickened heartbeat. He slid between her thighs and drove into her with precision. He was being careful, she sensed, careful of her pregnancy. 'The babies are fine, but I won't be if you stay this cautious,' she warned him.

And he took her lead, lifting her to him and driving deep, giving her the friction and urgency her body craved. It was a wild ride from there on in, her internal muscles clenching around him, glorying in renewed sensation, pleasure flaring up like a bushfire racing through her body. Exhilaration held her, that endless ache sated, but she still craved more. He gave it to her but the tumult of sensation was rising to a peak she couldn't resist and she climaxed again with a quivering cry of delight. He came to completion with a groan of satisfaction, his whole body jolting and jerking into hers.

'I like sex with you,' she said chattily in the aftermath.

Aristide burst out laughing, pulling back from her so as not to crush her with his weight. 'Of all the things to say,' he derided. 'You're a bossy little creature in bed, aren't you?'

'I'm only discovering that side of me and I could tell that you were moving into the "treating me like a delicate flower" approach and I wasn't having that,' she confided.

Aristide tugged the rumpled sheet over them. 'Go to sleep. We're lunching with Dad and Andy tomorrow at the taverna. It's a tradition when I come home. You and I will do a tour of the island first.'

Tabby stretched out and slept, gloriously relaxed for the first time in weeks.

The next morning, after a light breakfast, they set off in a classic open-topped green British sports car. His father was a classic car enthusiast and that particular one had been a gift for Aristide's last birthday. He used it to get around the island, which wasn't that large. It took only an hour to do a loop on the single main road that ringed Anthos. They stopped off at various places, walking along the beach at one point before climbing a wooded hill to the tumbled remains of an old lookout tower. From the hill they could view the whole island, taking in the little town with its ranks of houses on the slopes and the tall steepled church above the picturesque harbour and, finally, the luxury hotel resort built at the far end, which belonged to his father.

'So, you and Demetrius don't work together at all?' she gathered.

'No, he owns a luxury chain of hotels. We'll stop off there to eat some day.'

The taverna was right down on the beach and Tabby eased through the crush round the bar to choose a seat on the decking outside. She sipped her fruit juice and watched as Aristide dropped down into a seat opposite her. A woman was walking up the beach from the water, a sarong carelessly tied at her waist, a blue bikini top cupping her pert breasts. A mane of golden blonde hair drifted round her gorgeous face as a photographer ducked and dived all around her taking photo after photo of her. She peeled off the sarong and slowly turned, showing her perfect body and the bikini from every angle. She was both stunning and familiar. Tabby stilled, recognising her from the media images forever peppering newspapers and glossy magazines. Imogen Ross, the famous supermodel in the flesh.

'I think that's Imogen Ross,' she hissed at Aristide.

'It *is*,' he confirmed in an undertone.

'Aristide,' an English voice drawled barely a minute later. 'Introduce me to your little friend.'

Tabby's head spun back to the beach. Imogen Ross was standing in the sand by the edge of the deck and smiling at her while extending a manicured hand.

'Tabitha, meet Imogen Ross,' Aristide murmured without any expression at all.

The blonde gasped as she saw the ring on Tabby's finger. 'Oh my goodness, that puts *my* old thing to shame!' she exclaimed, waving her other hand to display the fabulous diamond solitaire she wore that flashed in the sunlight. 'I have a friend who tried to buy that sapphire at the auction last month. I didn't know you got it! How does it feel to wear a jewel worth millions, Tabitha?'

'Aristide... Tabby, your seats are waiting for you,' Andromeda Romanos called with a slightly desperate edge to her voice as she stood in the doorway of the bar.

'Excuse us, Imogen...'

'You were much friendlier when I saw you last night,' Imogen said with a reproachful look, her ripe red-tinted mouth settling into a disappointed pout.

'Goodbye,' Tabby murmured brittly as she turned away, feeling a little as though she might get a knife planted in her back.

Her brain was swirling in chaos. Aristide knew Imogen Ross? Why hadn't he warned her? Aristide had once been *engaged* to that beautiful woman? Or had she picked up that hint wrong? And was she really wearing a sapphire worth millions of pounds? Was that even possible? And had Imogen genuinely seen Aristide the night before? If so, why hadn't he told her about the blonde? Furthermore, exactly how had he come from a cosy meeting with the sickeningly gorgeous Imogen Ross and ended up making love to Tabby? She didn't like that time frame or the associations it awakened. Had she been the consolation prize? What on earth sort of a triangle had he got her into? And why the hell hadn't he warned her in advance?

'Of course, she knew we'd be here today for lunch because we arrived yesterday. Imogen is well acquainted with our family traditions,' Aristide framed glacially.

'Probably lying in wait for you like some poisonous jellyfish in the shallows!' Andy remarked with angry defensiveness. 'Ghastly woman—'

'Your ex...?' Tabby glanced at Aristide for verification as they took their seats at the table.

His dark eyes flashed gold with anger. 'For my sins. Yes.'

Tabby's slight shoulders set while her temper roared and boiled beneath her carefully tranquil surface. She was furious with Aristide for not telling her that they might run into his ex-girlfriend. She was even more furious with him for daring to have sex with *her* after spending time with his ex. She could never compete in attraction or appeal with a supermodel with perfect hair, a perfect face and an even more perfect figure. Any woman would cringe at such a cruel comparison, she reflected in exasperation, most especially a woman already conscious of her steadily growing and less shapely pregnant body.

Rescuing her appetite from that mood took time but by the time they reached the main course, she was eating again and chatting comfortably with Andy. She noticed that absolutely no one mentioned Imogen again, even though she entered the taverna and sat down with her photographer, talking in a rather loud voice in English about her diet and how she simply couldn't possibly digest cream or eggs. They departed, Aristide tucking Tabby into the car with careful hands.

Tabby sucked in a deep breath and flexed her engagement finger in the sunshine so that the light penetrated the pure deep blue of the sapphire. *'Millions?'* she stressed incredulously.

'My father collects classic cars. I collect rare jewels,' Aristide responded calmly.

Well, obviously, the very valuable sapphire would be remaining with Aristide once their engagement was officially over, Tabby reasoned as the car traversed the driveway to the large villa. Unlike Imogen, she would not still be flaunting a former engagement ring in the future, nor did she expect to. After all, she wasn't looking for expensive perks or rewards from Aristide.

They walked into the hall and Iola, Aristide's housekeeper, smiled and asked them what time they wanted dinner that evening.

'You decide,' he told Tabby. 'I'll be working.'

'Seven would be lovely,' Tabby told Iola with a smile, reckoning that she didn't need a thermometer to read Aristide's mood. It was definitely bordering on chilly.

He was in the dressing room getting changed when she got to their bedroom. 'So, that's it, then, is it? You're going to act as if nothing happened at lunchtime.'

Aristide straightened and zipped his jeans, wary dark golden eyes clashing unexpectedly with her questioning, open gaze. 'Nothing *did* happen,' he pointed out.

'Obviously, I'm going to ask about her,' Tabby replied defensively.

'But that doesn't mean that I have to answer.'

'I don't see why you wouldn't,' Tabby remarked, striving to be more casual about her curiosity. 'She came up and spoke to us.'

Aristide shrugged a broad shoulder as he pulled on a black tee. 'I don't owe you chapter and verse on everyone who speaks to us,' he countered very drily.

'No, but there's such a thing as explaining stuff to make people feel more comfortable...especially if we were to run into her again—'

Aristide straightened to his full intimidating height and the cotton tee dropped down, screening his spectacular muscled torso again. 'I can assure you that you won't run into her either in this house or my father's—'

Tabby nodded, fresh out of an alternative approach that wouldn't seem to be too much like prying. Of course, had she wanted to do that, she would have followed Andy to the cloakroom. She suspected that Aristide's stepmother wouldn't have had a problem telling her about Imogen, whom she had clearly disliked. But her self-respect cringed from the concept of going behind his back to find out information like a common gossip and his family would probably tell him what she had done anyway. She flushed with discomfiture, mortified that she had even thought of doing such a thing. Had it been Imogen who fell pregnant and miscarried? Tabby winced, grudging sympathy assailing her.

Aristide strode downstairs, marvelling at her curiosity. Surely it was obvious that he didn't want to talk about Imogen? Did he really need to say any more?

But Tabby was so blunt, so open, compared to the kind of women he knew best. He suppressed a groan and sat down at his laptop to catch up with his email.

Tabby lingered in the bedroom to change as well, throwing on a bikini and a wrap to take advantage of the pool behind the villa. Seriously, he wouldn't be looking at her and actually comparing her to Imogen, would he be? How did she know when he wouldn't even open the subject with her?

Having run him to earth in an obvious office space, Tabby hovered uncertainly in the doorway. 'Why won't you talk about her?' she asked.

Aristide narrowed glittering black eyes on her as she posed there. She looked so awkward and uncomfortable in her persistence because she knew that she shouldn't be pushing him. She was so unlike Imogen in every way and he cherished that even if it did make life more challenging. With her blonde hair lying rumpled on her shoulders, her make-up-bare face soft and open, she exuded honesty and good intentions.

'I just don't. Let's say it's a period in my life that I prefer not to revisit—'

'But clearly, if you were engaged to her, it was a major relationship that must've lasted a fair time. And if she is the one who miscarried your child, it must have been even more distressing."

Aristide jerked a shoulder in dismissal and swung away.

'Do you realise how much you're annoying me?' Tabby prompted.

An unwelcome smile slashed across his darkly serious features. 'Yes, I do.'

'I'm not going to fight with you about this...'

'Good, because you would lose,' Aristide told her equably.

'No, I wouldn't!' she tossed back to him, lifting her determined little chin in the air.

Aristide sent his chair screeching back from his desk and vaulted upright. He opened his arms. 'Come here, *angelos mou*,' he urged huskily. 'I want to kiss you.'

Tabby dragged in a shaken breath. 'You can't kiss me out of this!'

'You may be stubborn but I think I could.'

And he stood there, tall and dark and drop-dead gorgeous, a curl of black hair lying on his brow above the scorching dark golden gaze suddenly locked to her mutinous face.

'Try it and see,' Tabby suggested with a dangerous spark in her eyes as she moved closer.

Aristide could no more have stopped himself from reaching for her then than he could've stopped breathing. He hauled her to him and crushed her parted lips beneath his with a suppressed groan. All the turmoil in his busy brain stopped dead. The chemistry between him and Tabby electrified him, making him splay a hand across the soft curve of her bottom, jerk loose the sarong shielding her from him and yank her into full contact with the urgent thrust of his erection.

Low in her throat, she gasped as he enforced that connection and without hesitation he lifted her up and set her down on the edge of his desk.

Her body humming, giving her messages that she still wasn't used to receiving, Tabby blinked and then noted her surroundings, dismay and reluctance assailing her before embarrassment could cover her instead. 'Not here,' she said distinctly, struggling to suppress the hungry ache he had stirred between her thighs and rise above the sensation. 'And not when we're arguing either… I'm trying to talk to you.'

Aristide gritted his teeth, registering that he had underestimated her resolve. 'Tabby—'

'No, no more excuses,' Tabby cut in, sliding off the desk and snatching up her discarded sarong to wrap it round her hips again.

Aristide expelled his breath in a slow hiss and leant back against his desk, annoyance at her rejection, so rare in his experience with women, pulsing through him in a lethal wave. He tilted his darkly handsome head back. 'Ask yourself why I would have to tell you anything private about my past when we're only *faking* our engagement.'

Every scrap of colour drained from Tabby's once animated face. That reminder hit her like a brick and a much-needed wake-up call to common sense. Why? She had forgotten it was *all* fake except for her costly sapphire ring, and the shock that she could've allowed herself to forget such a basic fact reverberated through her like a crack of doom. No, she wasn't entitled to private explanations about his past loves, not if he didn't want to make them. And yet she had pushed and pushed until he ran out of patience and confronted her with the truth that she had been avoiding.

As she left his office, Aristide wanted to smash the wall with a clenched fist. He shouldn't have said that. Indeed, that was the very last thing he should've said when he sincerely wanted their engagement to become real. He had given way to temper, a rare occurrence with his deep, reserved nature. But he didn't talk about Imogen, not to anyone ever, not even his father. In truth, legally, he *couldn't* talk about her and she couldn't talk about him either, conditions his father had considered necessary at the time for *his* protection rather than hers.

And he was glad of his father's caution, wouldn't have cared to lift a tabloid newspaper some day and read *that* particular story. He wouldn't like the way it depicted him and couldn't help wondering just how differently Tabby would see him if she ever learned what an idiot he had once been.

And wasn't that truly *why* he had stuck to the letter of the law and remained silent?

CHAPTER SEVEN

TABBY MADE HERSELF walk out to the pool at the rear of the house and lie down on a lounger.

A mere minute later, she got up and dived into the pool, forcing herself into swimming fast aggressive lengths to drain her angry pain and tension away. No point letting feelings like that fester, she told herself. That wouldn't change anything. What she really needed to know right then was why she was so hurt. Aristide had merely reminded her of the truth that they were not a real couple where she would have been entitled to cherish certain expectations of him.

And in reality, he had hit the nail square on the head. Their engagement was fake, so how had she stumbled into a kind of non-relationship with the father of her unborn children? By not using her brain and thinking first, came the answer. The situation was of her own making. But you couldn't live for two long weeks as if you were involved in an endless one-night stand…at least, she couldn't. She wasn't built that way, wasn't able to just write it off as a casual, light-hearted fun fling. Certainly, there was nothing *fun* about the way she felt now. Her heart sank when she appreciated that all along, while she had been priding herself on her independence, she had been unconsciously hoping for *more* from Aristide Romanos. But he wasn't offering more, was he?

When she had had enough of the heat and was fed up with agonising, she went indoors and phoned her mother, catching up on her news. Lucia's treatment was going as well as could be expected at this stage. Guessing that it would raise her mother's spirits, she gave updates about her pregnancy and confided that she was currently staying in Greece with the father of her children. But no, she admitted, they weren't together-together, as she phrased it. They were only being civilised for the sake of things and meeting his family. There was no need to mention the fake engagement that had persuaded her to make the trip under false pretences, she reasoned ruefully. That was entirely her own fault. Aristide had extended the carrot and she had duly bitten.

She dined initially in solitary state that evening, Aristide joining her with apologies halfway through the meal. 'I'm also sorry for what I said earlier,' he added ruefully.

'Why? It was the truth,' Tabby replied with a determined smile.

'It is…and it isn't,' Aristide countered, striving to be more honest.

The urge to slap him surged inside Tabby and

she gritted her teeth, refusing to ask for clarity lest it make her seem too desperate for reassurance. She was here to oil the wheels for her children's future visits, to meet the family and let them get to know her. She was *not* here to romance Aristide. Aristide could keep his secrets. His past shouldn't matter to her because it was none of her business.

Aristide wondered how he had contrived to say the wrong thing *again* and he went back to work that evening even though he would've preferred to be with Tabby. When he went to bed, she was already there and asleep, the faint vanilla scent that always clung to her in the air. He lay awake so long resisting the urge to reach for her that he slept in long past his usual rising time. And Tabby was no longer beside him. When he got downstairs, he learned that she had had breakfast early and gone out. He frowned and questioned his security, sunning themselves on the veranda.

'She didn't want anyone with her. She said she fancied a walk.'

'You follow her to protect her even if she doesn't want company,' Aristide instructed and then his phone buzzed and an urgent business query made him turn away.

Tabby walked along the beach all the way into the little town, proud of herself for taking some exercise. When she arrived, though, she knew that she should've carried water with her because she was hot and a little dizzy, scolding herself for not thinking ahead, reminding herself that she needed to be more sensible now that she was pregnant. She walked off the beach, down the side of the taverna and into the front where a shaded terrace functioned as a snack bar. There she found a seat, fanning herself to cool down, and ordered water and a roll to sustain her on her return trip.

It wouldn't be a lie to say that her heart sank below floor level when she spotted Imogen Ross, impossibly tall and resplendent in a pristine flowing white sundress and hat, strolling towards her. Tabby turned her gaze quickly to the server who had returned with her order, keen not to catch Imogen's attention.

'No charge,' the server declared when Tabby persisted in trying to pay.

A frown on her face, Tabby returned her bag to the seat beside her just as Imogen took the seat opposite her. She noticed the server still staring fixedly at the table and, mainly, at Imogen.

'The Romanos family doesn't pay here and that ring on your finger means that you don't have to pay either,' Imogen explained in a tone of superiority.

Tabby wrinkled her nose. 'Not paying makes me uncomfortable.'

'Aristide owns most of the houses and the businesses here. What else would you expect?'

Imogen might be looking fantastic clad in her blinding white linen, glacial blue eyes deceptively languorous, but she reminded Tabby of a poisonous spider getting ready to pounce on prey. Although she had been enjoying the shade, Tabby lifted her bottle and her roll and began to rise to leave.

'Do I scare you that much?' Imogen rested her chin down on the heel of her hand, supremely poised and beautiful. 'Of course, I'm going to speak to you when I see you here. Please, sit down.'

Tabby hesitated and then, feeling foolish as she hovered uneasily, she dropped back into her seat again, her colour rising. 'What do you want from me?' she asked boldly.

'I want you to vanish and stop coming between me and Aristide,' Imogen replied with a pained note in her voice. 'I'm the love of his life and you are nothing but a pale facsimile of me. Have some pride... walk away—'

Another, more familiar masculine voice sounded without warning behind Tabby and made her jump. 'Tabby, I'm so sorry, I was held up.' Demetrius Romanos did indeed sound rather breathless. 'Let me get you into the car where you'll be comfortable,' he urged, reaching down to grab her hand.

'Aren't you even going to speak to me?' Imogen demanded imperiously of the older man.

Demetrius addressed her in low-pitched Greek at length and whatever he said made Imogen pale and look away. With that, he planted a supportive arm to Tabby's spine and walked her out to the classic Morris Minor sparkling with perfect trim and paintwork by the side of the road. 'I'll run you home. I was at the garage to collect a part I'd ordered when the taverna owner called me to tell me that you were here and that Imogen had cornered you.'

In another mood, Tabby would've laughed. All hands on deck and to the rescue, she thought hysterically. *A pale facsimile? The love of Aristide's life?* Admittedly she and Imogen did both have blonde hair and blue eyes, but Tabby's hair *was* paler and even her eyes were a deeper shade. Plus, she reflected without amusement, Imogen was much taller and skinnier as well as being breathtakingly beautiful. Competition? No, of course not, she wasn't entering any competition for a man and if Aristide wanted Imogen he knew where to find her, didn't he?

'Aristide's been looking for you all morning. He drove up and down the coast road in search but it didn't occur to him that you could have walked as far as the town.'

'It's a lovely walk.'

'Yes, but it's hot and you're pregnant,' he scolded in a fatherly tone that couldn't have offended her. 'I warned Imogen not to approach you again. That qualifies as harassment and she's legally bound not to harass any member of the Romanos family—'

'But I'm not a member of your family—'

'Yet,' Demetrius slotted in.

'Legally bound?' she dared to query.

'She caused trouble once before but fortunately she's rarely here. Her grandfather being ill put us all in this situation. Theo's not got long left.' Aristide's father sighed with regret. 'Once he's gone, however, she'll have no reason to return to the island.'

Other than Aristide, Tabby almost quipped, and

it was clearly Aristide who was her target and ultimate goal.

'So, Theo, whom you went to visit, is Imogen's grandad?' Tabby gathered.

'Yes, she's his late son's kid. When her mother died, she came here to live with her grandparents. She was twelve and she got into that modelling lark very young—*too* young, I suspect—but her grandparents didn't feel able to deny her the opportunity to make something of herself.'

'Well, she's certainly achieved that. She's world-famous.'

The classic car chugged up the steep driveway and, seconds later, Aristide stalked out to greet them, lean, strong face clenched taut with fury. 'Where the hell have you been?' he raked down at her from his vantage point on the top step.

'Don't you dare speak to me like that! I'm not a child who went out without permission and got lost!' Tabby fired back at him without hesitation.

Demetrius glanced between them, winced and climbed back into his car. 'See you both soon,' he called, unnoticed by either party, and drove off.

Tabby stalked up onto the veranda.

'I was worried about you!' Aristide exclaimed in his own defence. 'I went looking for you. I started worrying that you'd gone swimming in the sea and got into trouble. I've been frantic!'

'I walked into town.'

'In this heat? Why didn't you take the car?'

'I wasn't sure I'd be able to drive it. It has too many gears,' she complained, 'and I've only driven an automatic.'

'You should've had security with you, at least.'

'The worst thing that happened to me was meeting your ex again,' Tabby recounted, moving into the blessedly cool air-conditioned interior of the villa with a relieved sigh. 'And now I'm tired and I'm going for a nap—'

'How did you run into Imogen?'

'She approached me in the taverna and I'm not repeating anything she said. If there's ever a next time, though, she's getting a bottle of water thrown over her,' she threatened as she stomped up the stairs.

'I'm sorry. You shouldn't have to put up with her nonsense,' Aristide grated. 'She's my past—'

'Who still wants very much to be your present,' Tabby mocked.

'I think she just can't stand the idea of me moving on.'

But he hadn't moved on, had he? Not when he wouldn't even talk about his former fiancée. His father had told her more. He had shared Imogen's family relationship to the ailing fisherman, whom he and Aristide had gone to visit, and the telling fact that the gorgeous blonde had grown up on the island with Aristide. So, childhood sweethearts, Tabby could only assume. Was she right in assuming that Imogen was the woman in his past who had fallen pregnant and miscarried? Tabby was past wanting to know, past trying to talk about what *he* wouldn't talk about.

She reached the bedroom, kicked off her sand-stained canvas shoes and flopped down on the bed, rejoicing in the chill of the bed linen and the cool air.

Aristide strode in, curly black hair tousled as though he had been running his fingers through it, dark eyes fired up with angry defensiveness. 'Eight years ago, after I'd broken off the engagement, Imogen and I signed mutual non-disclosure agreements not to talk about each other. I stuck to the letter of the law with you. I suspect that was a mistake,' he breathed in a raw undertone, knowing that until that moment he had actually never *wanted* to tell anyone about Imogen. What was it about Tabby's angry, defeated aspect that tore at him to such an extent?

'When you actually *know* it was a mistake, let me know,' Tabby muttered tiredly as the phone in her pocket began an incessant ringtone. It was Violet's signature tune and, with a sudden flashing smile, she reached for her phone to answer it.' It's my sister. Can we continue this later?' she pleaded.

Aristide went into grudging retreat, more because she looked tired and drawn than because he wanted to back away. He wasn't doing such a great job of looking after her, he conceded grimly. Twice, she had been exposed to Imogen and had undoubtedly been abused or undermined in some way.

'So,' Violet began, all bubbly and upbeat and oh-so welcome in Tabby's ear, 'you're in Greece and not far away. We're holding a big flashy summer ball the day after tomorrow. Tore has offered to send a helicopter to pick you up—'

'But I've got nothing to wear!' Tabby gasped, her heart soaring at the welcome dream of being reunited with her sister, particularly when she was feeling so low and kind of hopeless about Aristide and his situation in which Imogen loomed large.

'I'll get you a dress. Can you be picked up tomorrow? Then we can have a girls' night before the ball.'

'So I'd be away just two nights?' Tabby chimed, suddenly awash with excitement. 'Yes, I think I could sell that to Aristide... It's not like there's anything much fun happening here. What time?'

The first Aristide knew about the summer ball in Italy was the sight of Tabby racing downstairs very much like an overexcited child, burbling about helicopters and dresses and seeing her sister and niece again. He was shell-shocked by the sudden rage that gripped him and burned like flames on his flesh. Tore freaking Renzetti, barging in with his offer of helicopters and fancy dresses on Aristide's territory.

'I'd only be away two nights,' Tabby bargained. 'You wouldn't miss me because you'd be working anyway.'

Boring old Aristide, slogging away at his laptop, while *his* woman danced the night away in some Renzetti-bought dress with Italian men!

'I will provide the transport and the dress,' Aristide finally cut in, burying the anger before it could betray him. 'And I'll be your partner for the ball.'

Her wide blue eyes widened even more. 'Oh...'

'I wasn't actually invited, was I?' Aristide guessed between clenched teeth.

'No. It wasn't a deliberate omission,' Tabby insisted. 'Violet didn't think. She would never be rude or unkind. Maybe I gave her the wrong impression of you and she thinks you don't go out and don't want to be put to the trouble of entertaining me here. I just feel like a break...'

Forty-eight hours and she needed a break from his private island and his company. Aristide felt as though she had punched him in the chest until he thought about all that had happened since their arrival. He had been a lousy host and a failure as a fiancé, but he fully intended to change that and level the score.

'Away...' Tabby waved an uneasy hand to indicate her need for an escape. 'Away from Imogen and the drama and the bad feeling and the arguments.'

'I'll organise it and arrange for some dresses to be flown over tomorrow for you to try. I've also got some jewellery you could borrow. You'll be the best-dressed woman at the ball,' Aristide declared with confidence. 'But before we go anywhere tomorrow, you ought to have your ultrasound and hopefully we'll find out the gender of our babies—'

Tabby's head was whirling. It had never occurred to her that Aristide would step up to make her dreams come true and wave a metaphorical wand like a sorcerer. She had even thought that that sort of glitzy occasion might not be to Aristide's taste and that he might be thankful to see her leave for a few days.

'It's too soon for the ultrasound again,' she told him. 'You're too impatient. We'll know eventually. It doesn't have to be right *now*.'

'We'll do it when we return, then,' Aristide conceded, although he could have admitted that he had already calculated every relevant date of her pregnancy, but it didn't seem to be the moment to confess that he couldn't wait to see how their twins were developing. 'Phone your sister back and tell her that *I* will bring you to their ball.'

'All right,' she agreed, unable to see how she could possibly dissuade him in their particular circumstances. 'I suppose it might look odd to your family if you let me go alone to something like that…and anyway, you ought to meet Tore, Violet and Belle as they're my family.'

'Do they know about our engagement?' Aristide enquired.

'Yes, but they know it's fake.'

'It's as fake as we want it to be,' Aristide contradicted, making her frown as she tried to work that answer out and came up unsatisfied, wishing that he didn't talk in riddles.

'I thought it was totally for show,' Tabby muttered uncertainly.

'I don't make that kind of commitment for show,'

Aristide asserted. 'I brought you here to work out whether or not we could be a real couple.'

Tabby nodded slowly. 'Like a sort of try-before-you-buy trial,' she assumed in a tone of gathering condemnation as her temper began to spark.

Aristide breathed in deep and slow before he spoke in a sudden driven rush. 'Please try to remember that you're dealing with a guy who made the most horrendous error the last time he chose to commit to a woman. Maybe he's been running scared since the moment he met you...'

At that unexpected speech, Tabby gazed up at him in unconcealed amazement and her anger drained away as though it had never been. In that moment, there was something so deep, real and emotional in Aristide's brilliant dark eyes that her heart pounded and her chest tightened. Imogen—the most horrendous error? Yes, she could get behind that opinion.

Running scared? Aristide? Of course, he would be apprehensive about getting seriously involved with a woman again. Afraid of trusting his own judgement, uncertain of what he had probably once been so sure of years earlier when it came to reading a woman's character. Having got it so badly wrong once, he was much more likely to walk the other way when it came to commitment. But it also went unspoken that she had to be the first woman to seriously attract him since Imogen and that was an intoxicating idea. Or was the truth far more prosaic? she wondered. He had got her pregnant. Would she ever have seen or heard from Aristide Romanos again if that hadn't happened? That was a more sobering thought and that fast she wasn't feeling intoxicated by Aristide any more.

'I shouldn't have shouted at you earlier,' Aristide commented over their delicious evening meal served on a deck overlooking the glimmering sea at his father's opulent hotel. 'But I was genuinely afraid that something had happened to you.'

'It's a flat beach and a straight walk into town. What were the chances of anything happening to me?' Tabby countered ruefully.

'Accidents *do* happen.' He shrugged. 'My mother tripped in her heels on the stairs and broke her neck—'

'But nobody could've prevented that,' Tabby reasoned in a pained undertone at that untimely reminder. 'That was a freak accident. Most would sprain an ankle or end up with bruises but they wouldn't die from it. Your mother was very unlucky.'

'How was I to know that you didn't go down to the beach today to swim?' Aristide shot back at her unanswerably. 'You didn't tell anyone where you were going or when you expected to be back.'

'You *didn't* know,' Tabby accepted, irritable at having to make that concession, dropping her blonde head while shooting him an accusing look. 'You just can't let me win an argument, can you?'

'And you can't stand anyone telling you when you're in the wrong,' Aristide completed drily.

That was true but torture wouldn't have persuaded Tabby to admit it to him. He had a mind like a steel trap and unforgiving principles.

'And this is why we're fighting,' she pointed out quietly. 'You like the last word—as do I. You can tell you're an only child. You've never had to compromise with someone different from you. You're a perfectionist. You won't consider human error or oversight as an excuse.'

'But I can change into a more user-friendly version of myself,' Aristide quipped with helpless amusement at the way she had summed him up and delivered her verdict. 'Only it won't happen overnight. It will take practice.'

Tabby stiffened. 'People *don't* change.'

'They mellow when they *have* to. It's the only way to build relationships with others. The art of compromise doesn't come naturally to me, but you know that we will both change when we become parents.'

There was an infuriating truth to that assurance. Instinct warned Tabby that motherhood would rearrange her priorities and alter her outlook. Hadn't she already watched Violet change as she grew into being Belle's mother? She surveyed Aristide, so achingly beautiful even in casual clothing. Even more beautiful *out* of them, a little inner voice reminded her, and she reddened as a flush of inner heat enveloped her entire body. She wasn't about to allow herself to think that way any more about him. That was a victim mentality, wasn't it? To imagine that she had no real choices of her own? And she was determined to choose a path that kept her safe from emotional harm or deep regret and, when it came to Aristide, that meant avoiding temptation and keeping the insanity of crazily good sex out of it.

'You have *another* private jet,' Tabby whispered as she boarded the sleek plane with its black upholstery.

'No, we're borrowing my father's,' Aristide informed her with amusement, watching her pick a seat in a whirl of impatient movement.

A helicopter had transferred them to the private airfield where his father kept his jet. Tabby was clad in loose linen trousers and a floaty pink top, blonde hair restrained to a neat braid down her slender spine, a slick of lip gloss her only concession to cosmetics. He had never known a woman so little concerned with her appearance. She barely glanced in mirrors, selected clothes to wear and pack according to practicality and could choose a ball gown from a rail of fabulous offerings in five minutes flat.

He had assumed she would spend the entire morning choosing her gown and deciding what to pack but she had packed before she came down to breakfast and had contrived to pick her gown for the summer ball before he had even left the room.

'Why are all the dresses some shade of blue?' was the only question she had deigned to ask.

'I love seeing you in blue and I have sapphires for you to wear at the ball—'

'Matchy-matchy. That's kind of controlling behaviour,' she had complained, shooting him a mocking wide-blue-eyed glance, teasing him because it was her favourite colour. 'What if I don't like wearing blue?'

'The next time, I'll take that possibility onboard and give you more of a choice,' Aristide countered without hesitation.

'Have you met my sister's husband before?' Tabby asked, finally settling into her seat opposite him.

'I've never spoken to him but I've seen him at events I've attended.'

'Violet said he's kind of a serious guy.'

'Most titans of industry are…goes with the territory.'

'I can't wait to see Violet,' she confided unnecessarily, her eyes sparkling at the prospect of the coming reunion. 'And Belle. She's walking now. I can't wait to see that either!'

'You like children,' Aristide appreciated.

'I've always liked them. I just didn't expect to have any of my own this side of thirty,' she confided ruefully. 'But I'm not thinking about that any more. It's pointless. I'm pregnant. The babies will eventually arrive and I will get used to the idea of being a young mother. If Violet can adjust to becoming a mum for Belle, so can I.'

CHAPTER EIGHT

AN SUV MET them at the airfield and whisked them to the Villa Renzetti. As Tabby sprang out of the car, a brunette hurtled down the shallow front steps of the imposing property and the sisters collided in a frantic hug on the driveway. They were talking nineteen to the dozen as Aristide left the car to greet their host, Violet's husband, Tore Renzetti.

'You won't see Tabby again until the ball,' Tore forecast, lowering the protesting little girl in his arms, who toddled off in the women's direction. 'Violet was so excited that her twin was coming that she couldn't sleep last night and she has so much to tell her that she was making notes in case she forgot something. I propose that we make our own entertainment. I'll give you a tour of this place and the village and we'll grab a quiet snack somewhere.'

There was a wild flurry of introductions as the sisters realised that they had forgotten their men. Tabby, now clutching the giggling toddler to her chest, gave

Aristide an apologetic smile over her shoulder as she followed her sister into the Villa Renzetti.

'This is a fabulous house,' Tabby told her sister as she scanned the sculptures adorning the classic splendour of the hall.

'Tore's into historic buildings,' Violet told her as she showed her into an inviting library, fired past a formal dining room and confessed that they hadn't yet furnished the drawing room. 'The ballroom is an amazing space and fully restored.'

It was indeed amazing, Tabby agreed as she walked the length of the big room, taking in the carved stone pillars being industriously wound in decorative flower lights for the following night. Caterers were bustling round the bar and buffet niche and she moved out of their path to walk out through one of the line of ornamental doors leading out onto the terrace beyond and into the fresh air. Stepping onto the gleaming tiled floor, where a scattering of pretty table and chair seating areas were being arranged, she walked to the retaining wall to take in the wonderful view. Miles of woodland met her appreciative gaze. Below the villa, she glimpsed the first buildings of the picturesque little village that her sister had mentioned was within walking distance.

'This is idyllic,' she told her twin.

'That's good because you're going to be a frequent visitor here,' Violet warned her. 'Let me show you upstairs to your room.'

'I wasn't quite sure what your preferred sleeping

arrangements would be,' her sister admitted awkwardly. 'So I played safe and put you and Aristide in adjoining rooms—'

'No, put him in with me,' Tabby surprised herself by saying boldly, but, when she thought about it, it made sense because she didn't like Aristide too far away from her. And why was that? And when had she started *feeling* like that? Possessive? Even a tad clingy? Wincing for herself, she reddened as she caught her sister's attention lingering on her.

'You've got attached,' Violet said worriedly.

'Yes...no...well, maybe a little,' Tabby conceded, crossing the beautiful bedroom her sister had prepared for her to take a sniff at the wonderful arrangement of fragrant peonies, lilies and roses in a jug on a table. There were magazines by the bed, a soft throw and a robe and mule slippers at the foot of it. Her heart warmed and lifted at the evidence of her sister's care for her. 'I did bring a dressing gown, you know.'

'Don't believe you. You always pack light and in a rush. So...' Violet paused with a meaningful look. *'Aristide...'*

Tabby froze. 'He's been very good to me. He takes an interest in everything, particularly in my pregnancy, but he's got a nightmare ex who casts a big shadow and screws stuff up between us. It's hard for me to know how I feel because I get so angry with him sometimes—'

'Hold it there,' Violet urged. 'We'll sit in the library. Stella will take Belle. I've got some smashing non-alcoholic rosé on ice ready for you. We'll talk until we're hoarse.'

Down in the cosy library, they curled up in comfortable velvet armchairs and talked behind a firmly closed door. The last thing Tabby wanted was for Aristide to learn that he was a topic of conversation. Snacks arrived and they nibbled and shared joys and grievances alike. They video-called their mother, delighted to see that their parent was feeling well enough to dress up and put some make-up on, and she was equally delighted to see her daughters reunited.

Only when Tabby mentioned the name of Aristide's ex did the atmosphere grow fraught between the sisters.

'Imogen Ross?' Violet repeated that name in unfeigned dismay. 'But she's starring in the fashion show being held before the ball—'

Tabby couldn't believe her ears. '*What*…fashion show?'

'This is a charity event and we have to thoroughly entertain the guests to bring in the numbers,' Violet explained. 'The evening kicks off with a trendy designer showing off her range and Imogen is the leading light of her show. She waived her usual fee for the designer, who's a friend of hers.'

Tabby rolled her eyes. 'My goodness and to think we could've offered her free transport here,' she mocked somewhat bitterly. 'Seat us somewhere at the back.'

'You're the one with the official ring on your finger. Hold your head high,' Violet contradicted. 'He broke up with her and you may not know the details but it was obviously a *bad* break-up if NDAs were required. What do you have to worry about?'

The four of them dined quite late that night, conversation waxing and waning until Tore and Aristide began talking business. Violet and Tabby returned to the library but not before Tabby took Aristide to one side and warned him that Imogen would be featuring in the fashion show. 'I asked Violet to seat us at the back out of sight—'

'No way. This ball is your sister's big night as a hostess and we have nothing to fear from Imogen as long as we stand together. If there's space in the front row, that's where we will be, *not* hiding!' he countered with derision.

Reassured by his adamant attitude, Tabby returned to the library. As the hour grew late, she was constantly stifling yawns, the travel and the excitement too much for her weary body and brain. Around midnight she parted from her twin, but her room was quiet and empty with no sign of Aristide's luggage. She stared at the connecting door between their rooms and sighed. She didn't know whether he had even gone to bed yet. The men had been talking of making a visit to the headquarters of Renzetti Pharma over dinner and she wondered if he had gone there even though it was late. That Aristide and Tore were getting on so well was great, she told herself. And Aristide couldn't be in two places at once, even if she missed him. Even so, she went to bed and slept the moment her head hit the pillow.

'I arranged for a hairstylist to come this afternoon if you want your hair done,' Violet told her over breakfast the next day.

'Lovely,' Tabby replied, but she couldn't hide her surprise.

'This my first official social event with Tore and I want to be turned out looking as sophisticated as I can,' her sister confided.

'Me too, especially with Imogen due to parade down the catwalk in the hall,' Tabby agreed.

'You have to show me your dress,' her twin carolled.

'It was love at first sight for me when I saw it and it fits like a glove so I decided it was meant for me.'

They took Belle down to the village and browsed the crafts before settling in at the café for more chat. Aristide was down at Renzetti Pharma meeting with some contact of Tore's who was looking for an investor. In the afternoon they went back to the villa to get ready for the ball.

Aristide knocked on the bedroom door, hating that that seemed necessary but, clearly, Tabby must've told her sister that she wanted a separate room and he was sentenced to polite distance whether he liked it or not. In fact, he really, truly did not like being separated from Tabby and he had barely seen her since they had arrived. As Tore had warned, she was preoccupied in catching up with her sister and her niece, their familial affection and closeness a palpable thing.

'Come in...why didn't you use the connecting door?' Tabby asked, a large towel wrapped round her middle, her wet hair concealed by another. Her pale skin, still bearing a damp glisten of moisture, gleamed and her shapely curves beckoned to him like a siren's call.

'What connecting door?' In demonstration, Tabby dragged open a door, only to discover that it did not lead directly into another bedroom but instead to a narrow servant staircase that, going by the dust and cobwebs, appeared disused and forgotten. 'My word, I wonder if Violet knows about this bit. Presumably that door opposite leads into your room.'

Aristide, sleek and dark and sexy in a black business suit, stepped past her to investigate and opened the door opposite to confirm that it was, indeed, his room. 'I didn't intend to disturb you, but I wanted to give these to you to wear tonight.' He passed her a large worn jewellery box. 'These belonged to my mother.'

'Didn't your father give them to your stepmother?' she asked in surprise.

'No, they're heirlooms from my mother's side of the family and they came to me.'

Tabby walked over to the window to sit down and open the box. A breathtaking river of large stunningly blue sapphires greeted her admiring gaze. The drop earrings were equally remarkable. 'These are antique.'

'They are. There wasn't time to have them reset.'

'They're fabulous just as they are. Are you sure you want me to wear them?' Tabby pressed uncomfortably. 'I'm not your wife.'

'I'm lending them to you for the sake of appearances.' Aristide downplayed his generosity with characteristic coolness, not encouraging her to read too much into the gesture.

'Thank you. They're absolutely gorgeous,' she said warmly, appreciative eyes skimming over his lean, strong face. The silence lagged, the atmosphere building as his brilliant dark golden eyes shimmered. He took a step forward.

And then a knock sounded on her door. It was the hairstylist and Tabby bid a harried, reluctant goodbye to Aristide before rushing off to pull on clothes.

Feeling flat out dissatisfied by that untimely interruption, Aristide departed again. And then he wanted to kick himself because he had also sought Tabby out to tell her about Imogen in advance of the fashion show but had somehow neglected to even open that conversation with her. He cursed, aware that his own reluctance to relive those years of blindness and betrayal consistently held him back from any desire to share the gory details.

A couple of hours later, Tabby was dressed, groomed far beyond her usual level and feeling as good as she could feel in advance of watching Imogen Ross star as the leading light on the temporary catwalk sat up in the vast hall.

Her dress was midnight blue, saved from being mistaken for black by the iridescent fabric that caught the light with tiny glimmers of green, purple and blue. It bared her shoulders and much of her slender back, cupping her full breasts and skimming her tummy, which was developing a pronounced curve. On her feet she wore high-heeled toning sandals and round her neck and dangling from her ears she sported the breathtaking sapphire combination, her hair swept up to show off her jewellery. Violet was wearing a ravishing golden sheath that enhanced her diminutive slenderness and a stunning diamond necklace glittered at her throat.

The fashion show was fun, typically full of outrageous garments that only a long-legged adolescent could have worn with panache. But here and there were little gems to be seen in the cut of a sleek red cocktail dress and a fabulous summer raincoat. Tabby tensed when Imogen strode down the catwalk towards them, flashing her spectacular smile. And she could see right there and then why Imogen was so famous because even the weird outfit she wore looked fabulous on her perfect body.

Aristide expelled his breath on a slow hiss and leant closer to Tabby to declare, 'I first met her when

I was fifteen. She was seventeen and already well known. I fell for her like a ton of bricks.'

'I imagine she was incredibly beautiful at that age,' Tabby muttered, looking at Imogen all those years on, still in full possession of her glorious looks.

'I changed my whole life to see more of her,' he admitted in a gruff undertone. 'I was at boarding school in England and I insisted on moving to one in Paris. I saw her every weekend and holiday for five years—'

'You were besotted,' Tabby whispered, grateful that he was finally talking to her but rather wishing he had chosen a better setting. 'Of course, you were.'

'I believed everything she told me, even when the story didn't fit. I ditched my critical thinking and intelligence. I was like a puppet on a string, providing the yacht holidays, the fancy hotels and the designer wardrobe, not to mention the photo opportunities she craved.'

'Why the self-hatred?' Tabby chided as the show took a break and refreshments were handed around.

'Because I should've known better. I grew up with women of that ilk, some of whom were my father's girlfriends, and yet I still didn't recognise those traits in her,' Aristide bit out, his lean, hard features grim.

Tabby skated a fingertip down a lean, strong thigh in reproof. 'Oh, stop beating yourself up about it,' she urged softly. 'Being young is supposed to be all about making mistakes and learning from them.'

'I may have been a fool for love once…but I will never be again,' Aristide framed in a harsh undertone.

'My goodness, you take mistakes too seriously,' Tabby told him briskly. 'You were very young and you idealised her and naturally you put her on a pedestal. I imagine you were the envy of all your friends with her on your arm and that your ego made you ignore the stories that didn't quite fit.'

Aristide dealt her a frustrated glance as if her relaxed attitude on such a subject was foreign to him. 'I trashed my relationship with my father over her.'

'And you both got over it and moved on, but now it's time to move on past the *whole* experience,' Tabby countered gently. 'You're such a perfectionist, Aristide, and you set too high standards for yourself. You were fifteen, you were still a kid when you made those choices, not an adult.'

'What mistakes did you make at fifteen?'

'I dyed my hair pink and it didn't suit me. Mum was furious and my school complained. I chose to study maths because I was good at it, not because I wanted to work in that field. I fell for the boy next door but he couldn't take his eyes off my sister even though *she* didn't know he was alive—'

'So, nothing came of it,' Aristide gathered.

'No, I grew out of him, got a crush on an actor instead. I think your problem likely was that you were a rich, probably spoiled and quite indulged kid, who had the freedom to make life-changing choices at too young an age,' she admitted. 'I didn't have those options and so my mistakes stayed small and relatively risk free.'

'At heart, you're very sensible and steady in a crisis,' Aristide remarked reflectively. 'You'll be a wonderful mother to our children.'

Just as the show kicked off again and the music fired up, Tabby looked at him and her heart pounded at the hot golden shimmer in his gorgeous eyes as they rested on her parted lips. The tip of her tongue sneaked out to moisten the sudden dryness there and with a muffled groan he reached for her, plunging his mouth down hungrily on hers. The teasing dance of his tongue against hers sent a red-hot burning shiver from her core up through her in a heated wave. A faint gasp was wrenched from her and she pulled back, her heart hammering inside her chest, her face flaming with mortified colour.

'You have no idea how much I want you at this moment,' Aristide growled in her ear before he leant back again.

And he had no very clear idea of how much she wanted him, Tabby thought ruefully, the heart of her burning, making her press her thighs together as if she could quell that wild craving. She reddened even more when she collided with her sister's amused smile and turned her attention back to the show's evening-wear selection.

The showpiece of the night was Imogen in her most unlikely wedding gown, a sort of goth-schoolgirl dress that bared her legs, those glossy brown pins of hers wrapped in ribboned white high heels. She looked spectacularly sexy, if not bridal, and the cameras flared and flashed all around them to capture her glamorous image. Her attention, however, landed repeatedly on Aristide, as if she was expecting to claim his attention, but Aristide was chatting away to Tore and looking nowhere near his former fiancée. And in that moment, Tabby's jealous insecurity fell away as if it had never been. She finally saw that Imogen might want Aristide back but Aristide was no longer interested. And though she might never hear the full story of their relationship, she no longer cared.

They moved as a party into the ballroom to allow the staff to return the hall to normal. As the music started up, Aristide tugged her beneath his arm. 'Now, at least, I can hold you close without exciting comment.'

He walked her onto the dance floor.

'There's nobody dancing yet!' she hissed in protest.

'So?' Aristide countered in challenge mode.

'I can't dance very well...people will notice,' she muttered shamefacedly.

Gazing to the side of his tall, powerful frame, she glimpsed Imogen beginning to strut her stuff on the floor, clad in something short, silver and very sparkly, a tall, older man in a smart dinner jacket matching her step for step. They were doing salsa or something, Tabby registered uncertainly.

'Who cares?' Aristide fielded, single-minded as usual.

'I care.'

'But why?' he replied unanswerably. 'You don't know anyone but your sister and husband here.'

'And she who shouldn't be named,' she muttered ruefully. 'She can dance too.'

'Ignore her... I do,' he said very drily.

She shuffled around the floor in the protective circle of his arms, drinking in the evocative scent of his skin, salt and musk and a hint of citrus in the combination. Slowly she closed her eyes, feeling him shift against her, realising that he was aroused and probably very much not up for any salsa dancing. That secret knowledge turned her on. Imogen was in the room and he wasn't looking in the blonde's direction and he wasn't craving her either. No, Tabby was the focus of his desire.

She shifted against him, rather suggestively. 'You... er—'

Aristide laughed, unholy amusement brightening his gleaming gaze. 'Of course. I've been in that state since the first moment I laid eyes on you in that dress. You look dazzling in it.'

'Thanks...'

And they danced and they mingled and had some supper before gravitating out to the freshness of the terrace, where the air cooled Tabby's overheated body. She breathed in deep, appreciating the faint chill on her exposed skin.

'I swore I wasn't going to ask but, er...what happened with Imogen and you at the end?'

Aristide grimaced. 'It was nasty. She told me she was pregnant and we got engaged. We set the wedding date and then my father came to see me. He was very upset and told me that I needed to get a DNA test done before I married her. She was the love of my life,' he bit out in a raw undertone. 'He told me that there had always been rumours that there were other men in her life but I was furious and I refused to believe him—'

'And that's when you had the big fight,' she guessed, wretched on his behalf that he had had so much faith in the woman he loved and had then had to live with the knowledge that he had been wrong in his every assumption.

'Yes. Initially I did nothing but my father's conviction that her child was not mine played on my mind. I lied to her for the first time,' he admitted uncomfortably. 'I told her that I needed a DNA test to ensure my child's inheritance rights and she insisted that she couldn't agree to one. That only made me more suspicious. I had her investigated and, sure enough, my father's convictions were proven. I confronted her. She lied and lied. Eventually she lost her temper and came clean. It wasn't my child and she already knew that, however she needed a husband for the squeaky-clean advertising campaign that was making her so much money. She couldn't be pregnant and unmarried without risking losing the contract.

I was simply…the fall guy. When I heard she'd miscarried some weeks later, I felt sad for all of us because at one time I had believed that child was mine.'

'I'm so sorry,' she mumbled, ashamed that she had pressed him. He must've been devastated by the discovery that his idol had had feet of clay throughout their relationship, that she had never really loved him back or been worthy of his trust.

'It's a long time ago but it screwed me up for a few years. I found it impossible to trust any woman,' he acknowledged tautly as he reached for her hand, his thumb stroking her slender wrist. 'Now can we sneak off and have sex in a broom cupboard or, indeed, any place? I'm feeling pretty desperate, *angelos mou*…'

'Er…' Mouth running dry at those images, Tabby stammered, not quite knowing what to say, wanting to agree but nervous of being seen or reported on and embarrassing her sister.

'Forget it for now,' Aristide advised on the back of a sigh. 'Your twin is making signals from the door. Obviously she wants to speak to you about something.'

Tabby walked indoors again with Aristide's arm wound round her like an anchor keeping her safe while she tried not to dwell on all that he had told her and all that she had deduced from what he had not said. It was enormously upsetting to finally have the confirmation that she had not been the first woman in Aristide's life to announce an unplanned pregnancy. Everything that had happened between them suddenly swam into clearer light from his angry, defensive outburst that first night when her contraception had let them down to his controlled and measured response to her eventual announcement. And yet, he had not once asked *her* to go for a DNA test to prove that her children were also his...

'What's wrong?' Tabby asked the instant she glimpsed her twin's deeply troubled face.

'You're not going to believe it but... Dad's here—'

'What?' Tabby exclaimed in disbelief.

Violet grasped her arm and drew her closer. 'Over by the bar wearing a loud blue velvet dinner jacket. He arrived as the guest of one of our VIPs, Mrs Soames. He's staying in her home. Apparently this week he's teaching an art class in Florence...'

'Oh, my word,' Tabby groaned, having turned pale at the news of her father's presence.

Aristide glanced across the ballroom to pick out the black-haired older man beside the bar. He bore not the smallest resemblance to Tabby. He was small, with Violet's darker colouring and a rather heavily lined and dissipated face.

'Our father, Sam Blessington,' Violet supplied. 'Artiste extraordinaire. A drunk, a wastrel and a wife beater. He's a horrible man. Tore wanted to ask him to leave but we don't want to offend Mrs Soames, who runs the charity we're raising funds for tonight.'

'Does he know that this is your home?' Tabby prompted.

'I'm sure he does. This is hardly his sort of event

but he's always keen to follow the smell of money and he must be broke right now if he's teaching an art class—'

'He can hardly expect any help from you,' Tabby responded. 'Just pretend you don't see him—'

'He won't allow us to get away with that. He likes attention. He won't let us ignore him,' Violet replied heavily. 'And if we try to, he'll cause a scene and there are a lot of journalists here tonight.'

'You can't let him blackmail us into letting him stay,' Tore said from behind his wife.

But even as her brother-in-law spoke, an almost forgotten oily male voice sounded behind them and Sam Blessington pushed forward to confront Violet with a sneering smile. 'Well, isn't this a surprise? I wasn't expecting to hear that my younger daughter is currently living in Italy with her new husband and within a few miles of where I'm currently staying—'

As Violet almost cowered, bad memories of their childhood clearly engulfing her, Tabby stepped forward, but Tore had already dropped a controlling hand down on her father's plump shoulder to steer the older man towards the door. 'Let's take this conversation somewhere more private,' he suggested calmly.

Tore directed their small party into the dining room at the back of the hall. 'Now, how may we help you?' he asked politely. 'I understand that you've neither seen nor spoken to your daughters since they were fourteen years old.'

'Then it's clearly past time for us to become reacquainted,' Sam Blessington declared, not one whit embarrassed by the truth that he had abandoned both his daughters as soon as he could. 'Particularly now when I'm going through a bit of a rough patch and could use a helping hand—'

'Not from us,' Violet sliced in thinly, lifting her chin. 'We owe you nothing.'

'We don't,' Tabby agreed, standing tall even as her father regarded her with unhidden distaste and resentment.

'You were always a bitch even as a little girl, taking your mother's side, answering back, refusing to give me the respect I was due—'

'Perhaps that was because you were beating up her mother...and *her*,' Aristide murmured without any expression at all.

'I think it's time for you to leave,' Tore interposed icily.

A crude expletive escaped Sam Blessington. Obviously drunk and out of control, he rounded on Tabby, cruel fingers biting into her arm as he gripped her and shook her violently while he screamed invective in her face. And the next moment, a shocking hush fell and her vicious father was lying flat on the floor, silenced and left unconscious by a punch. Tabby stared down at his prone body in disbelief. Aristide had moved so fast to silence her inebriated parent that he had simply blurred out of focus as he stepped between her and the older man to free her.

Tore opened the door to signal an employee and

returned to them with a serene smile. 'I'll have him driven home to Mrs Soames' villa. He was embarrassing her earlier and she'll be relieved to be free of him for an evening,' he surmised. 'I imagine that she's already regretting her invitation for him to stay with her.'

Pale as milk, Tabby turned to look at Aristide. 'You *hit* him—'

His lean, hard-boned face was taut, his dark golden eyes glittering. 'Yes. I would've preferred not to but he was in no condition to be reasoned with and I could not allow him to continue assaulting you or to cause you further distress,' he confessed in a roughened low voice.

'Thank you for stopping him,' Violet said shakily.

'Yes, that was done very neatly and quietly,' Tore interposed with approval.

But Tabby was still in shock at the knowledge that for the first time in her life someone had protected her from her father and he had done it without fanfare. Yet Aristide had had to employ violence, which she abhorred because the memories of her abusive childhood still haunted her in low moments: all the times she had tried and failed to safeguard her mother, the injuries they had both sustained during her father's assaults, the sick terror of knowing that nobody could stop him and that he wouldn't stop until he ran out of rage.

'I'm sorry about that,' Aristide reiterated as he guided her out of the room and across the hall to the ballroom, which was now heaving with dancing and chattering guests. 'I know how you feel about that sort of thing.'

'Let's go out onto the terrace again,' she whispered unsteadily. 'I need fresh air—'

'And perhaps some food?' Aristide said hopefully. 'You're very pale, in shock from that horrible confrontation. In fact I asked your sister if there was a doctor amongst the guests this evening—'

'Oh, for goodness' sake, I'm fine,' Tabby said defensively.

Aristide laced her fingers into his to raise her arm where angry purple bruises were already becoming visible. 'No, you're not fine and why should you be? That man is your worst nightmare and you never expected to see him again.'

Breathing in deep, Tabby dropped down into a comfortable seat on the terrace and he left her to bring her some food. A split second later, Violet dropped into the seat beside hers and gripped her hand. 'Are you OK?' she gasped. 'I'm so sorry. Everyone but Aristide just froze when Dad grabbed you. I wasn't expecting that but I should've done. Of course he always reserved the worst for you. You were always standing up to him—'

'*Trying* to,' Tabby corrected. 'That's why he hates me a little bit more.'

'I was like a little mouse around him, like Mum. I always hated myself for being so weak—'

'You weren't weak, you were understandably scared—'

'And tonight it was just like I was five years old again. I was terrified and I *froze*,' Violet groaned.

'He's gone,' Tabby soothed. 'And I doubt if he'll come back to visit.'

'Tore wished he had been the one to hit him but he was in shock. I hadn't warned him just how bad Dad could be—'

'Don't talk about it,' Tabby urged as Aristide reappeared and the fast beat of her heart steadied, her heart surging with sudden warmth and appreciation because he had sheltered her, even knowing that she would judge him for utilising force to intervene.

Aristide set out the food and she picked at it to please him because, in reality, she had little appetite. But the food and the tea took away the hollow feeling in her tummy and she began to relax again. The crisis, such as it had been, was over and she didn't want to make a fuss. He kept on checking her forearm, where deep purple bruising showed the indent of her father's fingers. 'I think we should get this cleaned up,' he said.

'No, the skin's not broken,' she protested, wishing he would forget the whole ghastly embarrassing scene that he had witnessed. 'Let's go and dance.'

Open surprise showed in his appraisal. She bore adversity well, Aristide reflected, made little of it, hated to be fussed over and yet that was all he wanted to do, along with wrapping her up in cotton-wool layers to ensure that nobody could ever hurt her again. He was still seething that the mother of his unborn children had been assaulted and denigrated before his eyes and that he himself had failed to see that more than a verbal attack was imminent. Sam Blessington, a man who had never learned how to control his temper, had bullied and victimised his wife and daughters until they had finally escaped his abuse.

Tabby drifted round the edge of the floor, calm in the circle of Aristide's arms. He smelled of wintry woods, crisp and clean and oh-so sexy and every time his thigh moved against hers, awareness flooded her and sent a delicious little shiver burrowing up through her.

'Was your father always like that?' Aristide asked.

'Grasping about money, yes. Violent when life goes against him, which it must be at the moment. I think he married Mum because her father was wealthy and he assumed he'd be a good bet but my grandfather was no fool and he refused to give him a penny. My father has a sell-out exhibition, spends all his money on the high life and then ends up broke again. He doesn't keep friends or girlfriends. He always turns on them and, unlike my mother, they don't take it. But give him a few months and he'll start painting again and reclaim his fame and his earnings. It's always boom or bust with him, nothing in between. Let's not talk about him any more,' she urged ruefully. 'I want to forget about him—'

'And your wish, *angelos mou*,' Aristide husked

in her ear as he lifted his head to look down at her, 'should be my command.'

As her gaze clashed with shimmering golden eyes, her heart started pounding hard inside her and a heated liquidity surged at her core. 'Then take me upstairs,' she whispered softly and she didn't have to ask him twice.

CHAPTER NINE

THE MINUTE TABBY'S bedroom door was closed, she crowded him back against it and stretched up over his glorious big powerful body to find his mouth for herself.

And the ferocious hunger that engulfed her was nothing she had ever expected to feel but it was there burning through her like a brand, driving her on. The taste of him, heaven knew, she *loved* the taste of him. He tasted like a banquet after she had been starving, the heat of the sun after an endless dark night. She couldn't get enough of the hungry glide of his tongue and the soft yet hard sealing satisfaction of his mouth.

Her hands sank into his silky black hair, tugging on it before dropping to his shoulders. He was wearing far too many clothes. She tugged at the jacket with impatient fingers and it dropped away just as she wrenched at his bow tie and embarked on shirt buttons.

'You want me,' Aristide purred. 'You *really* want me…'

'Pretty obvious, that, isn't it?' Tabby gasped, shaken by her own bold behaviour.

'No. The first time we were together, you were so restrained that I felt like a trial you had decided you had to undergo. Initially, I didn't understand your attitude, not until I realised that I was your first. But this is the very *first* time you have fully accepted the attraction between us and matched it…'

'Well, if you must be pedantic about it,' Tabby acknowledged defensively, not entirely happy to have put herself out there to such an extent.

'As much as you resemble an angel, you are also my little witch and the sexiest woman I've ever met,' Aristide growled with driven fervour as he claimed her parted lips with powerful hunger.

And the room fell away from her. In fact she felt as though, in a sudden move, she was being wrenched from her own protective skin and thrown into a new reality where she could shamelessly declare her own wants and needs as she never had before. And she would be secure in the knowledge that Aristide would deliver exactly what she wanted. His shirt fell away, leaving her free to spread explorative, worshipping hands over the bronzed expanse of his muscular, hair-roughened torso.

A groan was wrenched from Aristide and suddenly he was lifting her away, turning her round, lean fingers cool against her spine as he unhooked and unzipped her dress and it fell away in a splash of glittering darkness to her feet. She reached up to detach her bra, which an ambidextrous octopus would have struggled to remove, so devoted was it to upholding her pregnancy swollen breasts. He lifted her deftly out of her abandoned clothing and deposited her on the bed, standing back from her with scorching dark eyes while he shed socks, shoes and shirt and, finally, the narrow-cut trousers doing nothing to hide his arousal from her.

More daring now, particularly after being labelled the sexiest woman a notorious playboy had ever met, she slid back off the bed and dropped to her knees, peeling away the boxers and finding him with her hands, her tongue and her lips, listening to his breathing quicken and rasp in his lungs as she sought to give him the same pleasure he had given her. Long fingers settled on her head, guiding her, encouraging her. And then with a roughened, wordless plea he brought an end to her attentions and swept her up to return her to the bed with the sworn assurance that he had no intention of climaxing until he was deep inside her.

Her body tingled at the words, the heart of her already slick and desperately ready for him. She had never been as aroused in her life as she was in the moment he came over her and flipped her round onto her stomach and then up onto her knees. Almost simultaneously he moved behind her to find her tender exposed flesh with his mouth, his tongue and his carnal fingers. A low keening cry of arousal was dragged from her. Every touch he gave her only ratcheted up her tension and her ever growing need for more.

And then he was finally where she wanted him to be, pushing in, forcing her open, her inner sheath stretching to take him as he thrust forward with a growl of impatience that matched her own. From that instant of perfect fullness there was nothing but the wild thump of her heartbeat and the ever rising surge of excitement as he gave her exactly what she craved. Firm hands on her hips, he pounded into her and as she reached the pinnacle of her climax she threw her head back and cried out loud in ecstasy as the blissful release gripped her and roared through her trembling body to leave her slumped on the bed.

'You're always the first to leave the party,' Aristide complained, turning her over and coming down to her, sliding between her thighs and driving into her again with tender confidence.

And in the midst of the aftershocks of that initial orgasm, he taught her that she could still want more. Throughout, smouldering dark golden eyes held hers and it was an amazingly intimate experience to meet his gaze while the flexing power of his lean, powerful body shifted over hers and, ultimately, he surged inside her as he too attained release and groaned out his satisfaction.

In the aftermath, pleasure still lingering within her like an addictive drug, she was surprised when he continued to hold her close. She breathed in the scent of his skin with the sudden jarring acknowledgement that she had never been happier in her life and had never felt more at home. And that was the definitive moment that it became clear to her that she had contrived to fall in love with Aristide Romanos, the father of the twins she carried. She had thought herself safe and far beyond such emotional fantasies and yet Aristide was here and the more she saw of him, literally the more she wanted of him.

He splayed a big, possessive hand across her no longer flat belly and her heart sank a little because she didn't want to be snuggled only because she was the future mother of his children. She was much more keen to be held close and savoured because he wanted her and *only* her as a woman and a partner. But you couldn't have everything, she reminded herself stoically, already far too used to a world in which she had never received what she truly wanted.

Was she supposed to settle into being Aristide's occasional lover whenever he took the notion? Or was what they had actually heading towards a genuine destination? Possibly even a destination where the attraction between them would eventually fizzle out? She supposed that only time would tell.

After all, wasn't she on a trial to see if she could become a part of *his* concept of the perfect couple? Funny how it hadn't yet occurred to him that if she was on trial, *he* was as well. Strange how it hadn't crossed his mind that telling her he would only be a fool for love *once* was off-putting, rather than being a vote winner with the average woman. Who didn't want to be loved?

Imogen had been a user, enjoying his wealth, looks and influence and all the extras those attributes had brought her. But Tabby was different, very different. Even if Aristide lost all his money and power, she would still want him. After all, what she had never had, she couldn't lose or miss. No, she wanted Aristide for the fierce emotion and intensity he kept caged up inside him and was already showing towards the children she had conceived. He had so much to offer but he wasn't yet offering it to *her*.

Everything he had given Tabby was temporary or fake. Like their engagement and the jewellery she had worn at the ball. He was tender, caring and committed when it came to the children she carried but what about *her*? She needed *more* than lust, consideration and kindness. She was way too young to settle for anything less. And she wasn't about to change simply because she had fallen inconveniently pregnant to her one and only one-night stand. Or because she had fallen head over heels for him.

No, she wasn't going to be the adoring or slavish idiot who loved the unattainable guy regardless of whether or not he returned her feelings. She would sooner be alone and in little more than ten days she would *be* alone again, she reminded herself doggedly, back home in Violet's little flat and running the bakery. A return to normal life and the *real* world, she told herself, a first taste of being single and pregnant with nobody but her own family to fuss over her. It would do her good.

'I wish you didn't have to leave,' Violet lamented over breakfast.

'You knew I would only be here two nights. I'll see you next time you're in London,' Tabby declared with determined cheer.

'Only a couple of weeks until then,' Tore pointed out helpfully.

'But those will just be fleeting visits,' Violet sighed. 'We're thinking that we'll make this house our home base, particularly with Tore's grandparents and the Renzetti HQ nearby. It's the only move that makes sense.'

Aristide watched Tabby's face fall before she managed a smile to hide her dismay that her twin would be making her permanent home outside the UK. If he stayed with Tabby, he foresaw that it would be a necessity to buy a property in the same area but such a thought was very premature, he told himself impatiently. He was not prepared to redraft his entire future over the truth that she would be the mother of his children.

In addition, the three of them were barking mad if they imagined that Tabby would be back living in London in ten days' time. Aristide had never planned for her to return to her former life, scratching her living in that grubby little apartment while listening to customer complaints with a sympathetic smile. His care and protection of his unborn twins had begun the moment he was made aware of their conception and it naturally extended to Tabby's living and working arrangements. He didn't want her to work. He didn't want her tired or struggling alone while missing out on the best possible medical attention. That wasn't going to happen, he swore to himself. Her health and that of their twins were the top priority.

Tabby was damp-eyed parting from her sister and her niece. She and her twin had had long enough to thoroughly enjoy themselves but not quite long enough to cover all they longed to discuss in sufficient detail. Violet had recalled how weepy her late friend, Isabel, had been in the early months of her pregnancy with Belle and Tabby's brimming hormones seemed to be sending her down a similar road of emotional overload. Her eyes had even flooded with tears while Belle was watching a sad moment in a cartoon.

'You'll see your sister again soon,' Aristide informed her bracingly. 'I'll organise it but for the rest of your stay on the island, we're going to relax.'

'I've got no objection to that.'

'You like it on Anthos, don't you?'

'I'm not sure I'd like it the same in winter. I'm used to a bit of bustle around me.'

'I have many other properties in livelier destinations.'

Tabby had no idea why he assumed she would be

interested in the contents of his property portfolio. But he linked his hand with hers as he was ushering her back onto his father's private jet and her heart swelled with warmth inside her when he kept her anchored to him as they sat down. But while she was in love with him, he was not in love with her. She couldn't afford to forget those facts. She needed to protect herself. She recalled the wildness of their intimacy the night before and an inner flush of heat turned her pink as she inexorably relived certain moments, wondering if the sheer pleasure he gave her was normal, or if indeed she was somewhat oversexed. After all, she could barely look at Aristide's lean, hard features or meet those stunning eyes of his without thinking about what it was like when he touched her—*electrifying*.

Forty-eight hours later, Tabby had the ultrasound, which was done at the doctor's surgery in the village. The latest technology had been specially flown in for the occasion and was being gifted to the surgery, courtesy of Aristide. Her eyes stung like mad when she glimpsed the incredibly real 4D imagery of her babies. One was a boy, the other thought to be a girl. Aristide was fascinated, dark golden eyes ablaze with strong emotion.

'This makes them so real,' he said.

'But you do know that the gender is only a guess because it's still too early to be sure,' she reminded him.

'I read the small print just like you did.'

'We should've waited a little longer to have it done,' she reiterated.

'Why? They'll be here in little more than six months. We need to get ready for them. Rooms furnished, toys, staff hired,' Aristide counted out, galvanised by the concept of useful activity.

'They won't be needing their own rooms to start out. They'll be sleeping in the same room as me,' Tabby informed him calmly. 'A night nurse would be helpful the first few weeks but there will be no need for actual *staff*.'

Aristide breathed in deep and slow and opted to say nothing.

'Of course, I expect you were mostly raised by nannies,' she guessed.

'Yes. My father travelled round his hotels, which are all over Europe. He had no choice.'

'Well, I'm unlikely to be travelling very often.'

They dined that evening at his father's farmhouse and she got the official tour of Aristide's childhood home. Unlike Aristide's giant barn of a house, this one exuded warmth, atmosphere and comfort. Yes, sleek sophistication ruled in every corner of Aristide's imposing mansion, along with some very modern art, but it was not, by any stretch of the imagination, a *home*. Every choice Aristide had made screamed rich single male and the latest technology.

'Feel free to make changes to my house here,' Aristide told her calmly.

'I wouldn't feel right doing that,' Tabby replied,

even though she was bursting with ideas to improve the ambience. What they had was temporary and it wasn't her place to change anything within his home. 'It's not my house and my taste wouldn't be relevant.'

'It's the interior decorator's taste, not mine. I didn't need to be part of that process.'

The next morning was Imogen's grandfather's funeral and Aristide attended with his father. Andy had shown Tabby some pottery she had bought at an art gallery in town and she suggested they visit it some day. One day wended into the next seamlessly and Tabby relaxed again. Her morning sickness had dwindled and she stopped taking tablets to control it. Her appetite returned once she was no longer nauseous.

'I'm inviting some friends to join us on the yacht and we'll island-hop for a few days,' Aristide informed her.

'I didn't know that you had a yacht—'

'It's chartered out most of the time. I haven't taken a lot of time off work the last few years but that'll have to change when I become a family man,' Aristide remarked.

'You won't really be a family man. The children won't be living with you,' Tabby pointed out. 'Although I expect they'll come for longer visits once they're a little older.'

Aristide shrugged a broad bronzed shoulder. 'We can live together—'

Tabby tensed and paled at the casual manner in

which that invitation landed on her. Loving him made her very vulnerable and she had to be careful so that she didn't get too badly hurt. His whole approach was too casual to persuade her that he was serious. 'No. We're not drifting into some weird, loose live-in relationship just because I'm pregnant,' she warned him. 'I'm having these babies and getting on with my life.'

Aristide dealt her a startled, searching glance from shrewd dark eyes. 'I rather thought we'd moved beyond those boundaries.'

'No, this is just a holiday, not my real life,' she stated with conviction. 'I have to get back to my own life.'

'As long as you accept that that life includes me,' Aristide responded with studied mildness of tone, although he was not remotely as blasé about her answer as he was pretending. What did she mean about her *own* life? Did she mean she was planning to go back to dating other men? She was rather firmly rejecting his ideas. He had never asked a woman to live with him before! Didn't she appreciate what a major commitment that would be for him? No, she had just breezed on past the suggestion as if it hadn't happened, utterly dismissing it. He would've liked to go into the topic more deeply right there and then but a glimpse of the anxious tension etched into her small face dissuaded him from persisting just at that moment.

'We'll have a great time on the yacht,' he forecast soothingly, backing off. He was a terrific negotiator and he knew when to push and when to soft-pedal.

He wondered what was going on with her, wondered grimly if he should've put the whole business of his becoming a parent in his lawyers' hands. Should he have made it business rather than letting emotions get in the way? Legal advice would've given him guidelines. He knew his lawyers would disapprove of the actions he had so far taken: putting a ring on her finger, fake engagement or otherwise, bringing her to Anthos, letting his family get to know her. All of that was serious stuff.

It was true that he had done the same thing once before with Imogen but that had been at the point of a gun, when he had offered marriage even though he had felt far too young to make such a huge decision, only that very thought had seemed wrong, cruel and irresponsible when he had believed she was already expecting his baby.

Aristide was even more passionate than usual that night and Tabby submersed herself in the passion and refused to think about anything serious because she was so angry with him. As if she would simply move in casually with him because she was pregnant! That wasn't for her, that would never be for her. He had to want her for *her*, not for the babies inside her. She didn't want to stray into a live-in relationship with Aristide that then broke down because it was only a fleeting notion on his part. It infuriated her that Aristide did not see her as having choices when, in reality, she had nothing but choices to make.

The next morning, she was surprisingly calm over

breakfast on the veranda overlooking the cove. And there out to sea in deeper water sat a very large, opulent white yacht that was all sweeping decks and layers. 'Is that it?' she asked.

'Yes, my friends won't be arriving until the weekend so we'll have a few days alone first.'

'And then I'll be going home and all this…' she spread her arms in an expansive gesture that embraced the deep blue water washing the sandy shore below them, the fabulous house behind them and the yacht anchored in the cove '…all this will seem like a beautiful dream.'

Of course, it was different for Aristide because Anthos was home to him. But Tabby loved simply being with Aristide. He had so much power over her emotions that it frightened her. Didn't he realise that what they had found together was rare?

The following five days were a whirlwind of activity. She had packed with greater care than usual and at a slower speed, not wishing to find herself underdressed or missing anything once they were on the yacht. *Sea Breeze* was every bit as luxurious as it had looked from shore.

They sailed to Corfu, where Aristide took her shopping, strolling old cobblestoned streets between the historic Venetian buildings. She wore a classic cream sundress and the heat seemed to seep into her very bones, stealing her tension, making her work even harder to suppress the fact that soon she would be leaving the man she had recklessly fallen in love with. The day after that they landed on Rhodes, visited some ancient ruins and lunched in the medieval old town in a shaded garden. He insisted on buying her a new watch in a very upmarket shop where he was waited on as though he were royalty. The jewels on the face shone with blinding glitter in the sunshine that flooded the hotel room where he took her to literally ravish her in the late afternoon.

The uncontrollable hunger between them had not abated one little bit, in fact she thought it might be addictive so that surrendering to that overpowering desire once only made it easier to do again the next time it struck. It was like living a dream to have Aristide all to herself and to be the sole focus of his attention. As long as she didn't look into her empty future she was deliriously happy while she was still with him.

On Crete they walked the Venetian city walls, revelling in the fantastic views. On Santorini they watched a spectacular sunset and dined in a cliffside village where the views made her dizzy but the food melted in her mouth. It was idyllic and she was enjoying every moment of their time together. The boundaries between what was fake and what was real in their engagement seemed to have magically melted away.

But then she had deliberately let go of those boundaries. She had decided to make the most of their last week together and forget that theirs was a temporary arrangement. She had made the most of her happiness and his and would leave awash with wonderful memories.

On the fifth day Aristide's friends arrived, a married couple in their thirties, an Italian industrialist and his wife. Both were charming and great fun. They landed on Mykonos, lay on the beach and swam and then dined before taking advantage of the vibrant nightlife to visit a club. They rose late the next morning, sunbathed on deck while the yacht cruised on to Naxos, where Aristide's guests disembarked to travel home, and finally they arrived back on Anthos.

They breakfasted on the veranda, where she drank in the beautiful views, conscious that she was leaving that evening to return home and would presumably never enjoy that sweeping, stunning view of the sea again. There was an odd tension between them and then Aristide's stepmother drove up to take Tabby with her to the new art gallery in the village. Aristide looked mildly irritated by her arrival but did not object.

'I'll see you later,' Aristide remarked before stalking back into the house.

'Did I interrupt something?' Andy murmured, always intuitive.

'I don't think so, but I can't stay out long because I have to pack and I don't want to leave anything behind.'

'Where are you going?' Andy enquired with interest.

'Back to London this evening. This has been a

wonderful holiday but I have to get back to work,' Tabby replied.

'I rather thought that Aristide was hoping to change your mind on that score,' his stepmother admitted.

Tabby reminded herself that she was supposed to be Aristide's real fiancée as far as his family was concerned. 'Not much chance of that at the moment,' she said lightly, wondering if Aristide's father had been expecting a wedding announcement or something of that ilk before she departed again. It was best to play dumb.

'You know...' The older woman hesitated before continuing. 'Imogen left a lot of damage in her wake. He had such total faith in her and then that was ripped away from him and I suspect he has trust issues—'

'Don't we all?' Tabby countered without any expression at all but she meant it.

Aristide had trust issues, as did she, but hers had softened since Aristide had proved his reliability. But then she had already surmounted the problems of enduring a violent, unpredictable and uninterested father and her resulting innate distrust of men. Not all men were the same. Sam Blessington was just a bad apple in the barrel. But essentially she had moved on under her own power to embrace the best life she could make for herself without letting herself be restricted by the unhappy events during her childhood and adolescence. Aristide still had to make that leap and she couldn't do it for him. He needed to move forward alone, willing to change for her benefit.

They entered the gallery, Aristide's stepmother immediately leaving her side to go upstairs in search of the owner, who was sourcing a specific metal sculpture for her husband Demetrius' birthday. Tabby lingered by the pottery, which was Violet's particular love, but she could see nothing unique enough to attract her twin's acquisitive urge. The door behind her opened, the tap-tap of stilettos making her turn round and then wish she hadn't.

Imogen, clad in a very sleek black dress, aimed her megawatt famous smile at her, golden hair shimmering in waves round her slender shoulders. 'Oh, this is convenient. You've saved me from having to visit my landlord.' Scooping keys from her trendy little bag, she extended them. 'The keys to my grandparents' cottage. I'm returning them as per the agreement.'

'They're nothing to do with me,' Tabby said uneasily.

'Oh, don't be silly. You're *living* with Aristide, aren't you?' she pressed, tossing the keys, forcing Tabby to catch them. 'I wish you well of him. He'll never love anyone the way he loved me.'

Tabby lost colour and turned away. 'Goodbye, Imogen.'

Andy came clattering down the wooden stairs to the rescue and Imogen turned on her heel and stalked out, the door slamming on her exit.

'What am I supposed to do with these?' Tabby shook the keys in exasperation.

'Celebrate. She must've finished clearing the place and now she's leaving.' Andy sighed in relief. 'Now we won't be running into her all the time.'

CHAPTER TEN

TABBY SETTLED THE bunch of keys down on Aristide's desk in the room he used as an office. 'I ran into Imogen at the art gallery and she insisted that I return these for her.'

Aristide grimaced. 'I'll return them to the agent. She shouldn't have approached you with them, but I'm pleased to know that she's finally leaving and that she will have no reason to return to the island.'

'I'm going upstairs to start packing before lunch—'

'I'm heading down to the beach for a walk.' Aristide rested his truly stunning dark golden eyes on her shuttered face. 'Join me...'

'OK,' she said lightly, determined to keep up the bright, breezy front out of pride. 'But I'll have to change first into something cooler. I dressed up for Andy this morning. She's always so elegant.'

Up in their bedroom, where she scolded herself for even thinking of it as *their* bedroom, she picked out denim shorts and a halter top and stripped off her skirt with its elasticated waist, loose-ish top and flat comfy pumps, thinking enviously of Imogen's racy red stilettos and bag and of how frumpy she herself had felt in comparison. She didn't want to leave Aristide but she had to protect herself.

Aristide was already down on the beach, a tall, lean figure sheathed in black denim jeans and tee, thumbs lodged in his belt loops as he gazed out to sea, his proud profile perfect in silhouette. She followed the path down to the shore, recalling the rarity of beach visits while she was a kid and the sheer excitement of seeing her first rock pool. Her throat thickened and she swallowed convulsively as she looked at Aristide and then looked away again. Like Imogen, she was leaving and, certainly, with regard to the remaining months of her pregnancy, Aristide would be a very rare visitor...if he visited at all.

Refusing to hurry herself, she strolled across the sand to join him, her flip-flops abandoned above the waterline. 'It's so beautiful and peaceful here,' she sighed appreciatively.

'I don't want you to leave,' Aristide admitted with absolutely no lead-in.

'I sort of don't want to leave either,' she confided reluctantly. 'But isn't that always true of a good holiday?'

'Don't cheapen what we've had together,' Aristide rebuked. 'We've enjoyed a great deal more than a shared holiday.'

Tabby stiffened. 'Yes, we've had a fling and now it's over,' she opined in a tight, small voice. 'But from now on we will be friends and co-parents and that's a bit of a jump right now, but not seeing each other until the babies are born should make it easier on both of us.'

'I don't know where you get the idea that I'm about to vanish from your life while you're pregnant. What sort of male would behave like that?'

'A sensible one. Get a little distance. Obviously if I'm ever in need of help I can phone you…or if… er, anything were to go wrong,' she muttered. 'But we're not together in the normal sense of the word.'

'I thought we were,' Aristide declared.

'Did you really?' Tabby turned to look at him, her wide blue eyes bright against her breeze-stung cheeks. 'Put it this way—if you thought we were a couple, you failed to mention it to me.'

Faint colour etched the knife-sharp slant of his high cheekbones as he reflected that that was a fair point, for he had, out of habit, played his cards very close to his chest. 'I did tell you what I was hoping to achieve by bringing you here with me.'

'Yes, that this was a trial run at a real relationship for you. One mistake, Aristide. I'm nobody's *trial run*. I didn't come here to try and impress you as an eligible match like some desperate Regency heroine. I came here because it made sense to find out more about my babies' father and his family because you and your family will soon be part of their lives.'

'You're very defensive,' Aristide growled, dark eyes glittering with censure.

'No, I'm not. For once, I'm simply being honest. We're both adults, we're both pretty practical and we're not enemies. That's a fair basis for being good co-parents in the future.'

Everything she was saying was inside her head and came from a logical place, but her heart was breaking at acknowledging the current emptiness of her future without him. She wanted him and she loved him but he did not feel the same way about her, unless she had got something terribly wrong in her assumptions.

'You've detached from me. You're talking as though you've already gone.'

'I'm being sensible. We had a great time together but now it's almost over,' she argued, conscious that he had hit the nail squarely on its head with that accusation. Once she knew that she was leaving, she had tried to move on mentally from him, but what else could he have expected from her? Nothing would ever persuade her that Aristide would have preferred an emotional scene in which she condemned him for using and discarding her.

Aristide moved a step closer and reached for her hands. 'I didn't want to do the conventional thing. The dinner, the down on bended knee and the proposal felt outdated to me when there's already a ring on your finger. I now see that I was too proud, arrogant and smart for my own good. I should've given you the frills,' he completed.

Tabby had been stunned into silence. Out of the

blue, he was asking her to marry him? Where had that come from? She hadn't foreseen that, should've seen that coming from a mile away, she reasoned. She had formed her attitude to him of recent entirely on what he'd shown her. And what she realised at that point was that Aristide had shown her *nothing*. Well, at least nothing that even hinted at love.

'I wouldn't need frills from a male that sincerely cared for me,' she muttered awkwardly, her tongue tripping in her dry mouth because the unexpected had thrown her for a loop.

'Obviously, I *do* sincerely care for you,' Aristide reasoned.

'Yes, but you don't love me.' Tabby said it for herself, the truth of that statement piercing her like a sharp, wounding blade.

'We don't need love. We have everything else,' Aristide told her fiercely. 'We have the passion, the fun, the commitment, the caring. How could you possibly add to that?'

Tabby winced at the fierce grip of his strong hands and he released her crushed fingers immediately. '*I* need love. I'm happy for you that you don't care about that but I do care about it. I will only marry a man who loves me and whom I love. It's the one thing I can't compromise on. I don't think a marriage that isn't built on love would survive the years. Love keeps you loyal to your partner even when that partner is annoying you. Relationships wax and wane and go through rough patches,' she argued. 'But what keeps a couple together is love.'

Aristide shrugged a broad shoulder, his lean, darkly handsome face stony. 'I don't agree with that. You're getting all emotional and this isn't what this is about. Marriage is primarily a legal agreement—'

'I don't agree with that either. I will only marry a guy who can tell me he loves me...and be proud of the fact,' Tabby retorted chokily, her throat convulsing. 'But you're never going to do that. You're still too bitter about Imogen—'

'I am not... Why the hell are you bringing *her* into this?' Aristide demanded with sudden anger.

'Because she's right there square in the middle of it whether you like it or not. I'm not saying that I believe you're still hung up on her but I do think that your attitude is all wrong because of your experience with her. I also won't be punished, with your lack of faith in me or in love, for her mistakes either. I deserve better. Thanks for the proposal, Aristide, but no, thanks.'

'Tabby...' he breathed rawly, hands hanging fisted by his sides.

Tabby spun back to him. 'And don't think I don't know that you're only thinking of marriage because I'm pregnant,' she condemned. 'It wouldn't even have occurred to you otherwise. And that's humiliating, Aristide. Maybe I'll never meet anyone who loves me or wants to marry me, but I need to stay free to give life a chance. If I married you I'd be closing myself off to the possibility of being loved by someone else, someone who is less of a perfectionist than you and who can care about me, flaws and all!'

As she stalked away in high dudgeon, wondering if she had dealt as poorly with him as she possibly could or whether she should have reacted differently, she suppressed her increasing emotional turmoil. Right, she reminded herself, it's time to pack. If he couldn't give her even a faint prospect of love, she didn't want him, she told herself firmly. Such a marriage would end in tears.

He might fall for someone else. And she truly did not fancy figuring as the loving wife of a male who did not love her back, who would always refuse to let the more tender emotions have space inside him. It would be like downsizing herself, reducing her to the level of a beggar seeking crumbs from the table. She would end up hating herself if she married a man who didn't love her.

Aristide was in shock. He had been toying with the option of marrying Tabby almost from the first moment he'd learned that she was pregnant. It had lurked in the back of his mind ever since. Of course, he hadn't told her that and it had never crossed his mind that a proposal in such circumstances could be seen as humiliating. He had been more afraid of recklessly talking himself into a sudden disastrous marriage that had no prospect of success. And then he had got to know Tabby properly and appreciate her and, no, he was not always looking at her and seeing flaws. Where had she got that idea from? In fact he thought she was pretty much perfect, which would no doubt surprise her.

But instead of proposing marriage at the start, or at least making his intentions clear, he had instead conned her into a fake engagement and done himself no favours, he registered belatedly. And, of course, that had been a total con on his part, knowing how attractive he still found her, knowing how much he wanted her in *his* home and *his* care and *his* bed and away from other men. In truth he was very possessive of her and the thought of having to let her go away from him and back into the wider world downright appalled him.

Not only had he let that fake-engagement business get in the way, but he had also let Imogen get in the way. He should've shared that story with Tabby much sooner. He had even let a desire to be cool and real get in the way! So, you propose on a walk along the beach on her very last day! Couldn't you have done better than that, Aristide? Waiting until the eleventh hour and going with casual had been a major miscalculation.

He breathed in deep and swallowed back his disordered emotions with difficulty. He had royally screwed up, although he was still trying to work out how a proposal of marriage could be humiliating, offensive and too little too late. And she was upset, deeply upset. She had gone pale and there had been a bleak look in her eyes he had never seen there before.

'At least come home with me tonight,' Aristide urged as his limo swept away from the airport.

It was a dreary wet night and she was back in London. She had been surprised when Aristide had announced that he was flying to the UK with her.

'I need to get back to work too,' he had told her.

'Why would I come home with you now?' she asked him baldly.

'You're returning to an unheated apartment that contains no food. It would be easier for you to return to my place instead.'

'There's a twenty-four-hour supermarket within a mile of my place. I'll manage...but thanks for offering,' Tabby told him, striving to be gracious even in the face of adversity. And it was definitely adversity when you turned down a marriage proposal and the guy just went on being charming and considerate. If he'd brooded, acted short-tempered or ignored her, at least she could have convinced herself that he or his ego had been damaged by her rejection.

She eased her gorgeous engagement ring slowly off her finger. Her fingers had swelled in the heat so it wasn't that easy an operation and when it was finally free, she extended it to him.

'I don't want it back. I bought it for you.'

'Stop being difficult!' she exclaimed. 'I'm tired, I'm hungry and on a short fuse.'

'Then why don't you come home with me?'

'Will you please stop being nice?' Tabby launched at him furiously. 'It's only making this more difficult!'

Aristide studied her flushed and mutinous face

with concealed amusement laced with concern. He wanted to gather her into his arms and soothe her. Hangry was a word that had been invented for Tabby when she was tired and hungry.

'And please take the ring...' she begged, still holding it out to him.

He dropped it into a pocket. 'I don't want it.'

'Well, sell it, then,' Tabby muttered, aware that she was behaving badly and embarrassed that she couldn't control her heaving emotions just then. She didn't want him to sell her ring because she adored it, but it wasn't hers to keep and she wasn't mercenary. 'I'm sorry I left the box on the island.'

She climbed out of the limousine and went to open the door but he stole the key from her hand and opened it for her while his security men saw to her luggage, hauling it upstairs. Aristide moved ahead of her, switching on lights, and the emptiness of the rooms engulfed her along with a bone-deep sense of loneliness. More than anything she just needed to phone her sister and admit her misery and when feeling as low as this, she consoled herself, she could only go up.

Aristide looked frustrated, glorious dark golden eyes troubled, and guilt almost got her by the throat. For the first time she saw that he wasn't much happier than she was and he was showing it. Just last night she had been in his arms and as close to him as any two human beings could be and now that seemed like a far-off daydream.

'I'll see you tomorrow,' Aristide announced.

'But I'll be working—'

'No, you won't be,' Aristide contradicted. 'Violet was unable to find a replacement for you willing to take on the contract for less than a month, so you still have two weeks to fill…unless, of course, you want to break the contract and pay the costs.'

Tabby gritted her teeth. She hadn't known that her replacement was in the bakery to work a full month and she had no intention of taking any action that could damage her sister's business or add needlessly to her costs. Slowly she nodded, wishing that just once Aristide didn't know better than she did. 'Goodnight,' she said tightly.

'Tomorrow morning, I'll send the car to pick you up at eight,' he specified. 'We'll have breakfast together and we can talk.'

'We've got nothing left to talk about.'

'I'll talk. You can listen and pronounce judgement,' Aristide traded lazily.

Tabby resisted the temptation to tell him that she wasn't a judgemental person, because it would have been a lie where Aristide was concerned. She watched every move Aristide made, tried to read his every expression and was forever judging him and making assumptions. Now she was learning that, just as often as she was right, she often got him wrong. The shock of the marriage proposal she had refused was still reverberating through her.

She ordered food from a local takeaway place and

ate before falling into bed, exhausted and miserable because it was very bad news that she was *already* missing Aristide.

What on earth did he think they still had to talk about? The very prospect of that dialogue made her anxious because she didn't want to argue with him again. What did she have to say to a male who believed that love was not required in marriage?

She was collected on the dot of eight and driven through the heavy morning traffic to Aristide's apartment. In spite of everything that had happened between them, the anticipation of seeing him again made her heartbeat quicken and released butterflies in her tummy. She breathed in deep as she crossed the threshold.

Aristide was elegantly dressed in a dark business suit. His lean dark face was taut and a touch remote. But he was still so hot he positively sizzled with lethally sexy vibes. His expression reminded her very much of their first meeting at her former place of employment and she shrank a little into herself, asking herself what else she could've expected, other than distance, after turning down his proposal. She doffed her coat, passed it to his hovering manservant, and took a seat at the table.

'I'm going to do most of the talking,' Aristide warned her in advance. 'Try not to interrupt me until I'm finished. I get one chance at this and one chance only. I don't want to screw it up.'

Slightly dazed by that unexpected speech, Tabby

nodded and reached daringly for a croissant as her tea was poured for her. 'You're making me nervous,' she whispered, the atmosphere so tense that her stiff shoulders already ached.

As the door closed behind his staff, Aristide released his breath in a pent-up hiss. 'I grew up in a very dysfunctional household. Women floated in and floated out again. I often had no idea whether the same woman would still be there on my next visit and there were often frightening arguments and distressing scenes between my father and his partners. All of that made me decide that I would ideally settle down and marry one woman and stay with her for ever...'

'Understandable,' Tabby chipped in and then flushed, for she remembered him saying that she was to let him speak.

'I never planned on being a playboy. Imogen did that to me. I didn't trust women any more. I protected myself to the extent that, when I met you, I was as tempted by you as I was by the conviction that I should turn away and walk fast in the opposite direction...because the moment I met you I knew that you would mean *more* to me in every way. And that scared me, made me feel out of control. But I couldn't resist you...'

Tabby unfroze and glanced up, her anxious eyes warming with acceptance of that admission. 'The same,' she echoed, feeling that identical irresistible pull tug at her afresh.

A sudden slashing grin stole the gravity from

Aristide's lean darkly handsome features. 'I just can't shut you up, can I?'

'Probably not,' she agreed, her cheeks burning.

'I told myself that it was only one night, but even over dinner that first evening I was toying with the idea of spending the whole weekend with you, which was groundbreaking for me.'

Tabby sipped her tea, wondering where he was heading in his journey back to the start of their relationship. It was definitely heartening to learn that long before they'd reached the bedroom he had already been interested in spending more time with her. 'And then the contraceptive misunderstanding occurred and it all went horribly wrong,' she said for him, because that subject had already been done to death and she had long understood why he had reacted the way he had that night.

'That night, if you hadn't given me the impression that you were cheating on your fiancé, I would've been in touch and apologising for my loss of temper by the next day. That's how keen I was on you,' he volunteered, disconcerting her.

'So you waited…'

'Had you investigated—'

'Came to check me out,' she filled in. 'And I told you that I was pregnant without meaning to tell you.'

'When I suggested we fake our engagement, I was already thinking of marriage. I never planned to let you go. I was deceiving you.'

'And you're admitting that?' Her eyes were wide

with surprise and a certain amount of satisfaction because the idea of marrying her had been in his head long before he had actually got around to proposing.

'I'm a talented negotiator.' Aristide snatched in a deep, audible breath. 'I was so busy plotting how to catch and keep you, I didn't consider how my...er... unconventional courtship would look to you.'

Tabby startled both of them by bursting out laughing. '*Unconventional courtship?* Yes, that's a term and a half!'

'That ring was always intended for you—'

'But you didn't ask me to marry you, Aristide.' Tabby shot him a reproving look. 'In fact the closest you came to that was asking me to live with you.'

Aristide gritted his even white teeth. 'I was still committed to the softly-softly approach where our lives would eventually be so entangled you would wake up one day and realise you couldn't live without me—'

'You *hoped*,' she slotted in, unimpressed.

'And then you said no when I asked you to marry me and it all fell apart. I didn't know where to go from there. I had nothing more to offer,' he admitted in a raw undertone. 'And I can't face my life without you in it...so quite happy for you to chip in now with useful suggestions.'

'Why can't you face your life without me?' Tabby asked squarely instead, her heart beating very, very fast because Aristide was severely on edge, ferocious tension etched in every hard line of his lean, strong face.

'Well, it's got almost nothing to do with you being pregnant! I wanted you, *seriously* wanted you, long before I knew you were pregnant. That simply complicated everything and gave you the wrong impression. Why would you think I only wanted to marry you because you were pregnant?' he shot at her. 'We could've done that thing with co-parenting that you kept on throwing at me. We could've just shared a house. But *only* if you marry me are you mine and it's very important to me that you are mine and nobody else's!'

'Why?' she asked again.

Unconcealed frustration radiated from Aristide. 'Obviously because I *love* you…why else?' And after a moment's hesitation, 'Should I have said that first?'

Tabby was reeling in shock. 'But yesterday on the beach you said you didn't believe love was necessary.'

'I would've done almost anything rather than acknowledge it because, in my experience, once you tell a woman you love her you are no longer equals and she *owns* you!' he framed in raw condemnation.

Her lips parted company. 'I've got to admit that I wouldn't mind owning you body and soul,' she confided softly.

'Since when?' Aristide queried in a tone of disbelief.

'Oh, from just about the first moment I met you, and that desire got stronger every time I saw you. So, there you are, I'm your worst nightmare come true. I would own you if I could,' she confessed in a rush with a huge smile. 'I tried to fight how I felt about you too but it didn't get me very far. I'm not being facetious but my love was at its height when you punched my father and shut him down. I like how protective you are.'

Aristide almost knocked a dining chair over as he swooped on her and lifted her right out of her seat. 'I'm crazy about you, *angelos mou*—'

'Me too…about you, I mean,' she mumbled blissfully, colliding with burnished golden eyes that made her heart sing with happiness because now she could see the tenderness and the very real feeling there. 'So, let's own each other and then never mention it again. And I won't marry you until Mum's back in the UK because she's got to be part of it.'

'But we're getting married, right?' Aristide checked with a huge smile. 'All I had to do was tell you that I loved you and then you wouldn't have said no?'

'Sometimes the uncool, simple way is the best move you can make but you will always try to be clever and make it complicated, Aristide.' Tabby ruffled his curly hair with fond fingers. 'That's just the way you are.'

'Can I take you straight back to bed?'

'Only if you let me sleep late afterwards,' she bargained. 'That was too early a start this morning.'

He carried her through the hall and down into his bedroom and laid her on the bed. She looked around, remembering their first encounter in the same room and giving him a sunny smile because all that nonsense and drama and insecurity were now far behind them.

'Being owned is paying dividends I never expected,' Aristide teased. '*Thee mou*, I love you so much I can't wait to put a wedding ring on your finger. Oh, that reminds me...' Reaching into his pocket, Aristide extracted her engagement ring and slid it onto her finger. 'That feels better.'

'Why did you never ask me to take a DNA test?' she enquired with belated curiosity.

'I didn't have the slightest shade of doubt that if you were pregnant, it was my child. I knew that you were very different from Imogen. When I consider it, I was already trusting you back then without even realising it,' he murmured with wry amusement.

Tabby yanked on his tie and sat up to kick off her shoes. 'Why are you still wearing clothes?' she asked with a distinctly sultry smile. 'Well, you already knew I was bossy—'

'Be warned. I am bossy too.' Aristide stripped without hesitation, dropping everything in an untidy heap.

Tabby shimmied her hips out of her skirt and peeled off her top. Aristide's eyes literally lit up when he caught a glimpse of her full breasts cupped in lace. 'You look amazing.'

'I didn't think I'd be back in this bed today.'

'I love you,' Aristide breathed in a roughened undertone. 'I'll do whatever it takes to make you happy. You'll have no regrets.'

'You're already making me happy.' Tabby tugged him down to her and they kissed and she luxuriated in the connection of their minds and warm bodies. He felt like home. She should've guessed he loved her in the way he made love to her, she reflected. He had shown her love in so many little ways and she hadn't counted them up when she should've done. Only a male in love was so tender, thoughtful and caring round the clock. As they joined together with a kind of frantic energy, the world around her splintered and she lazed in the aftermath in his arms, feeling ridiculously happy and content.

'We'll fly over and visit your mother and set a wedding date if it's possible.' Aristide was back on target and laying down the law, his attack of humility short-lived.

'We'll see,' Tabby sighed, wondering if he would ever learn patience.

'You're always going to call me out when I get too big for my boots, aren't you?'

'Probably,' she agreed sleepily. 'But it's good for you to be challenged.'

EPILOGUE

Five years later

It was a divine dress. A slinky red sheath that flattered her curvier shape since her pregnancies. Of course, it would never surpass her old favourite that she had worn at Violet's first summer ball in Italy. Aristide had persuaded her to wear it again the previous year and it had enjoyed various other fashionable outings but this year Tabby had decided to be different and wear something a little more daring, now that she wasn't pregnant any more.

Every year they attended Violet and Tore's charity ball. They were able to bring the children with them since Tore had extended the house into former outbuildings at the rear. And the kids had a lot of fun as well when they were in Italy. It was a blessing that their children were all so close in age. Tabby's twins, Elias and Eleni, were four, just like Violet's twins, Sofia and Enzo. And little Xander, their two-year-old toddler, followed the others around like a faithful puppy. Belle, Violet's adopted daughter, was incredibly sensible even at the age of six and she watched over them all, preventing the worst excesses.

Tabby had been grateful when she had had her twins, because she had found the pregnancy tough, and Aristide had persuaded her into Xander, a pregnancy that had been a breeze in comparison to her first. Three children were enough, she had told him, although she knew he still had hopes that she might change her mind and Violet being pregnant again would probably make him a little envious.

Tabby, however, was perfectly happy with the family they already had. Elias was dark-haired like his father, inclined to be bossy and serious. Eleni was a blonde dreamer, never more content than when she was reading picture books to her dolls with a made-up storyline. Xander, with his rampantly curly black hair, was just an ever moving splash of liveliness and endless chuckles.

They had held their wedding in Greece at the village church. For the first time their giant house on Anthos had been filled to the gills. Her mother's cancer was in remission, but it had taken considerable encouragement to get her out to Greece because she hated travel and rarely left her home outside London, which she had inherited after their grandfather died, along with a comfortable income. Both Violet and Tabby were regular visitors to the UK and still saw their mother often.

The mansion on Anthos was now their home base.

Tabby had found the island an amazingly relaxing place to raise young children. Demetrius and Andy were very much involved with their grandchildren and the kids had much more freedom to run wild on Anthos, much the same as Violet's kids did on the Villa Renzetti estate in Tuscany. And when the sisters wanted to get together, Tore had come up with a solution. He had gifted Tabby and Aristide a piece of land nearby where they had built a modern, comfortable holiday home. They often used it at weekends, but for big occasions like the summer ball they stayed at the villa itself because it was more fun for the kids to be with their cousins and there was constant supervision there.

Tabby had done without hiring a nanny. She wanted to enjoy her children while they were young, spend time with them, appreciating that it wasn't time she would get back and there was never a shortage of babysitters around her. Not least Violet, who adored her nephews and niece almost as much as she adored her own children. After the ball, Aristide and Tabby were flying off for a week of precious alone time on the yacht and leaving their children with their aunt and uncle.

Aristide, long since dressed ahead of her, strode into the bedroom and stopped dead. *'Thee mou,'* he husked. 'That's a killer dress.'

Tabby pirouetted in front of him. 'You like?'

Aristide grinned down at her, the warmth of his

gaze heating her down deep inside. 'I will like taking it off on *Sea Breeze* even more...'

'One-track-mind male,' Tabby quipped as he tugged her back against him and dropped a careful kiss on an exposed shoulder.

'No, a very happy male. I love having you all to myself,' he confided. 'Is that selfish?'

'No. Tore and Violet do the same. We're not only parents, we're a couple and we mustn't lose that in family life. We need a break now and again.'

'Well, you do all the heavy lifting,' he conceded, turning her round, pressing a kiss to her brow, careful to steer clear of her make-up and her hairdo. 'I want to rip your dress off you, *angelos mou*. It's incredibly sexy and it will be torture looking at you in that all evening and not being able to touch you. Maybe I am a male with a one-track mind...'

'Whatever you are, I love you,' she murmured, suddenly frustrated that she couldn't kiss him and risk messing her make-up.

'I'm absolutely crazy about you. You rock my world,' Aristide groaned. 'It only took me almost twenty-nine years to find a woman who could teach me how to be happy.'

'I didn't know real happiness either until I met you,' she confessed softly.

* * * * *

If you couldn't put Her Two Greek Secrets,
*then be sure to check out the previous instalment
in the Billion-Dollar Bride Swap duet,*
Unveiling the Wrong Bride!
*And why not try these other stories
by Lynne Graham?*

Baby Worth Billions
Greek's Shotgun Wedding
Greek's One-Night Babies
His Royal Bride Replacement
Shock Greek Heir

Available now!

Get up to 4 Free Books!

We'll send you 2 free books from each series you try PLUS a free Mystery Gift.

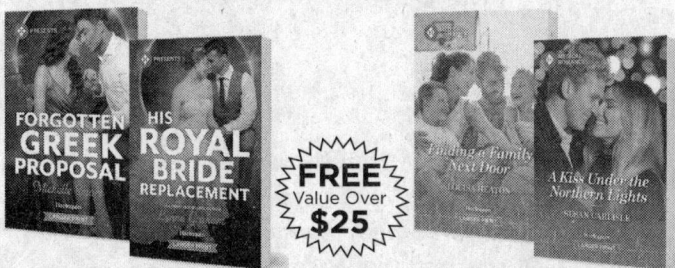

Both the **Harlequin Presents** and **Harlequin Medical Romance** series feature exciting stories of passion and drama.

YES! Please send me 2 FREE novels from Harlequin Presents or Harlequin Medical Romance and my FREE gift (gift is worth about $10 retail). After receiving them, if I don't wish to receive any more books, I can return the shipping statement marked "cancel." If I don't cancel, I will receive 6 brand-new larger-print novels every month and be billed just $7.19 each in the U.S., or $7.99 each in Canada, or 4 brand-new Harlequin Medical Romance Larger-Print books every month and be billed just $7.19 each in the U.S. or $7.99 each in Canada, a savings of 20% off the cover price. It's quite a bargain! Shipping and handling is just 50¢ per book in the U.S. and $1.25 per book in Canada.* I understand that accepting the 2 free books and gift places me under no obligation to buy anything. I can always return a shipment and cancel at any time. The free books and gift are mine to keep no matter what I decide.

Choose one:
- ☐ **Harlequin Presents Larger-Print** (176/376 BPA G36Y)
- ☐ **Harlequin Medical Romance** (171/371 BPA G36Y)
- ☐ **Or Try Both!** (176/376 & 171/371 BPA G36Z)

Name (please print)

Address _____ Apt. #

City _____ State/Province _____ Zip/Postal Code

Email: Please check this box ☐ if you would like to receive newsletters and promotional emails from Harlequin Enterprises ULC and its affiliates. You can unsubscribe anytime.

Mail to the **Harlequin Reader Service:**
IN U.S.A.: P.O. Box 1341, Buffalo, NY 14240-8531
IN CANADA: P.O. Box 603, Fort Erie, Ontario L2A 5X3

Want to explore our other series or interested in ebooks? Visit www.ReaderService.com or call 1-800-873-8635.

---

*Terms and prices subject to change without notice. Prices do not include sales taxes, which will be charged (if applicable) based on your state or country of residence. Canadian residents will be charged applicable taxes. Offer not valid in Quebec. This offer is limited to one order per household. Books received may not be as shown. Not valid for current subscribers to the Harlequin Presents or Harlequin Medical Romance series. All orders subject to approval. Credit or debit balances in a customer's account(s) may be offset by any other outstanding balance owed by or to the customer. Please allow 4 to 6 weeks for delivery. Offer available while quantities last.

Your Privacy—Your information is being collected by Harlequin Enterprises ULC, operating as Harlequin Reader Service. For a complete summary of the information we collect, how we use this information and to whom it is disclosed, please visit our privacy notice located at https://corporate.harlequin.com/privacy-notice. Notice to California Residents – Under California law, you have specific rights to control and access your data. For more information on these rights and how to exercise them, visit https://corporate.harlequin.com/california-privacy. For additional information for residents of other U.S. states that provide their residents with certain rights with respect to personal data, visit https://corporate.harlequin.com/other-state-residents-privacy-rights/.